BILLIONS
OF VIRGINS IN ECSTASY

The Memoirs of Strange de Jim

In the beginning…

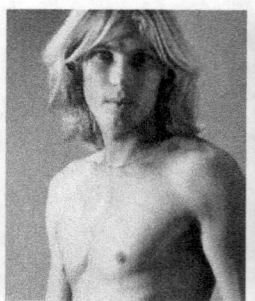

Oops! Watch Out!
Here Come the Secrets of True Love and the Tingly Portions

Hi, I'm Strange!

Would you guess, from looking at me (be honest now!), that I could find a hundred wonderful friends, including these, happy to tell the public they'd enjoyed undressing and receiving a blindfolded Strange massage from yours truly?

I'd accidentally stumbled upon half the secret of True Love. Then I gave Strange massages to thousand of other men and women, all ages, sizes, shapes, colors and persuasions. What I found startled me so much that it took me years to believe what was right under my fingers. I realized we're all just folks, and everyone's tingly portions are perfectly fine. Through this acceptance I was able to tap into the sex drive, the greatest energy in the universe. The results were pure magic.

Zelda, Jason and Fifi.

I myself was whisked away to Beverly Hills, where I teamed up with eccentric erotic healer Fifi Fulbright Bo-ku. We both fell in love with two Angels raised without shame, Zelda Mishimoto and Jason Tolliver McVeer. Last night, on a brilliantly lit white marble stage, with a live audience of two thousand and billions watching from home, we four led the whole world to a shimmering Orgasm of Light.

Should you learn our secrets? Is it safe to set *Billions of Virgins in Ecstasy* loose in a world-class Imagination? You'll do as you think best, of course. Here's how it all happened.

Strange de Jim
I Grow Up and Find Half the Secret of True Love

I was born to write. From the start, when grownups asked me what I was going to be, I told them, "Author!" What kind? "Famous." That wasn't the half of it.

I was named Strange, so I was told, after my father's sense of humor. Dad always made everyone laugh with silly quips and practical jokes, and I was a cheerful little geek, always singing and making funnies. So the name stuck.

I grew up in Charleston, West Virginia, as the son of the chief accounting officer of Atlantic Greyhound and his wife. Until my fateful meeting with the Baroness Ethelina von Elm a year ago, it never occurred to me to question that they were my real parents.

Besides being a geek and a goofball, I was naturally a little brainiac, always first in my class. In junior high I won a tennis letter and was student council vice president. In high school, not to brag, I was editor of the school paper, winner of a National Merit Scholarship and, most fun of all, emcee for the school talent show.

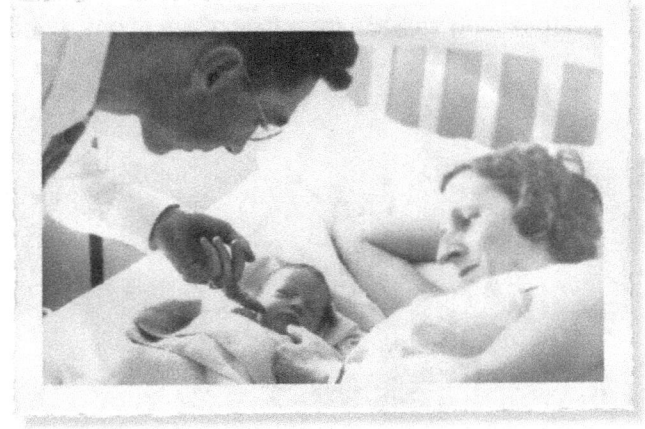

A Strange is born, with his alleged parents.

The worst thing that happened during my entire childhood was that my Mom died of cancer when I was in sixth grade. I remember Dad dressing my brother John and me in suits and taking us down to the hospital. I was embarrassed that the nurse was right there listening as we said our last goodbyes.

After a long motherless year, Dad started dating, and my brother and I were all for her. Each Saturday, while Dad was golfing, she'd take John and me to the movies and then out for a Blossom Dairy hamburger and ice cream soda. At her house or our house, it was, "Can I fix you boys a sandwich, get you something to drink?"

My brother and I started asking, "When are you two getting married?" When we got home from the wedding I asked for a sandwich and was told I was a lazy good-for-nothing who could fix it himself. She never took us to another movie.

Between this nasty turnabout and my mother's death, you can see how Trust would become such a central part of my life's work. But I wouldn't really figure that out until much, much later.

I was in the throes of adolescence, and had more urgent things to handle. Until I was in junior high all my erotic fantasies were about girls. Then I saw some high

A Strange Christmas, 1955.

school boys playing basketball with their shirts off, and in an instant realized I was bisexual (though I didn't dare have sex with another male until I was in my twenties). I wasn't appalled to find I was also attracted to guys. It felt as right as with girls. I just knew I had to keep it secret.

My dad died after my freshman year at college. For a while I tried to follow in his footsteps, collecting an MBA from Columbia, and working for five years as a management consultant in New York . That's where I developed my impressive sense of style, and a certain *je ne sais quoi* with the ladies.

But I didn't really hit my stride until 1971, when I moved to San Francisco. That's where my part of this story really begins.

My main squeeze for about a year and (right) with my roomie's fiancé.

I Become San Francisco's Town Fool

On September 17, 1972, the most beloved and powerful person in San Francisco was Herb Caen, lead columnist of the *San Francisco Chronicle*. Later in life he would win a Pulitzer Prize for his daily reports on the sights and sounds that made the City by the Bay such a magical place. On this particular day, he told his million-odd readers, "Strange de Jim reports: 'Since I didn't believe in reincarnation in any of my other lives, why should I have to believe in it in this one?'"

On a whim I'd sent the quip, and Herb and I proved godsends to each other. He loved zingers, and I loved seeing my name in the paper. Over the next quarter century he ran hundreds of my items. They were mostly just little silly musings. Here are a few typical examples.

Bottoming out: I have this young friend who calls himself Strange de Jim and who is–well–different. Like: "Today," he'll say, "I mourned the loss of Ephemeral, my soap bubble. Once you've named them, you hate to see them burst."...Or, "Last night I folded paper until I reached origami."

"Monogamous," foolosophizes Strange de Jim, "is what one partner in every relationship wants it to be."

Our roving elegant, Strange de Jim, was in top form while dining at Le Trianon. After the sommelier had gone through the uncorking, sniffing and pouring ritual, Strange swallowed the obligatory mouthful, looked up and declared triumphantly, "Wine, right?"

Strange de Jim

Strange de Jim browsing Dalton's bookstore at Sutter and Kearny, noticed that Shelf Number 28 is labeled "Sex & Etiquette," and murmured, "Just watch the hostess—that's always been my rule!"

During the "Yes on No on Six" benefit at Chez Jacques, Strange de Jim was asked his sexual preference, and I'm afraid he replied, "The Mormon Tabernacle Choir."

[During a drought] "I suppose all this rationing is necessary," muses Strange de Jim, "but I for one feel very foolish saving up water for a rainy day."

It was at artist Satty's party for Jack Nicholson that Strange said to the star, "I saw you in *Gone With the Wind*, and you were just great." Jack, very straight: "That was Clark Gable." Strange: "Same difference." (Nicholson is not ready for Strange de Jim, but who is?)

Everyone read Herb's column, so wherever I went, people already knew me. To protect my anonymity as a mystery character, I wore a tasteful pillowcase over my head at public functions. Here I am on the **dais at a Herb Caen Roast** (above right) at the Mark Hopkins Hotel. I hosted **Strange de Luncheons** (above left) every Friday at Enrico's on Broadway, in the notorious topless section of North Beach. All the guests had to wear pillowcases or the equivalent over their heads. The local hoi polloi loved it, and so did I. Really, only one thing was missing in my life.

I Touch Naked Bodies, Oodles and Oodles of Naked Bodies

My public life was roaring along. But my private life sometimes left something to be desired. Ah, it can be lonely at the top. Plus, it's hard to get a decent date when you're always wearing a pillowcase over your head.

By way of resolving that issue, my good friend April talked me into going to massage school. "You'll get to touch naked bodies," April pointed out.

April Smith

I signed on the dotted line.

The only time I'd really thought about massage was while reading *Kim* by Rudyard Kipling. One day Kim was utterly exhausted and receiving a massage from a rich Indian woman and her niece. "And the two of them," Kipling wrote, "laying him east and west, that the mysterious earth-currents which thrill the clay of our bodies might help and not hinder, took him to pieces all one long afternoon–bone by bone, muscle by muscle, ligament by ligament, and lastly, nerve by nerve. Kneaded to an irresponsible pulp, half hypnotized by the perpetual flick and readjustment of the uneasy chudders that veiled their eyes, Kim slid ten thousand miles into slumber–thirty-six hours of it–sleep that soaked like rain after drought."

Who wouldn't want to learn how to do that?

After graduating from the Massage Institute of California, I bought a massage table, started inviting people to lie on it, and began oiling my way into Hog Heaven. Both men and women would actually undress and let me rub them all (or almost-all) over.

"Correct me if I'm wrong," was my opinion, "but isn't this the smoothest dodge ever?" Massage wasn't full sex. It wasn't romantic love. But it was delightfully close. Massage is where healing, sex and pleasure meet, an ideal place to learn about True Love. (I might have learned about True Love sooner if I'd concentrated more on the healing, but I'm not embarrassed to admit that, being human, for me it was mostly the pleasure and sex.)

As a teenager, when I'd been making out with girls, as we were kissing, I'd move my hands towards their breasts, and they'd push my hands away. A little later, I'd move my hands towards their breasts again, and again they'd push my hands away. I'd keep trying until they quit pushing my hands away, and from then on, breasts would be inbounds, and my hands would start heading south for the winner. I wasn't really pushy, but I was still persistent. As far as I knew, that was the way all guys were supposed to operate.

Now, years later, I'd adopted the same sort of strategy in massage. When I offered people massages, it was almost always because I was attracted to them, and, during the massage, I'd include their tingly portions if they'd let me–gently returning after a verbal "no" or physical pushing of my hands away. Often, my partners' bodies would take over. They'd become aroused and let me bring them to a happy ending. However, they'd be reluctant to return for a second massage. That, of course, taught me an important lesson. *Try harder to have sex the first time, because it might be your only chance*. I had no idea there might be a better strategy. Meanwhile...

I Learn Magic

The seventies in San Francisco were a magical time. Some people even took to teaching how to make everyday magic in strange new ways. While sampling a lot of New Age groups, I started attending Wingsong workshops led by Lisa de Langchamps, the ethereal lady you see here.

Lisa de Longchamps

We'd sit in a circle, holding hands. Each of us would make a wish. Then we'd close our eyes, breathe healing energy through our chakras, and believe our dreams into reality.

What are chakras? I'll explain them in more detail shortly. For the moment, let's just say said chakras are seven delightful, swirling energy centers conveniently located within the average human body. Each one has its own special color and sound, and energizes a different kind of reality.

Lisa's main teaching concerned "manifesting" our wishes by picturing them clearly in our minds and then breathing loving energy up our spines and lighting up our chakras.

One important rule was that if the wish involved another person, we'd always add, "...if it's the will of his or her soul." Respect for every other human is one of the non-negotiable parts of True Love, and I thank Lisa for making this so clear.

Sometimes it seemed that miracles occurred–big miracles, like spontaneous healings and sudden gifts of emerald rings. Other wishes seemed to fizzle. So was there magic or not? To this day I'm not sure.

You can test the Wingsong techniques for yourself. With Lisa's blessing I published her teachings in a book called *Visioning*. It went through four printings of five thousand copies each. And

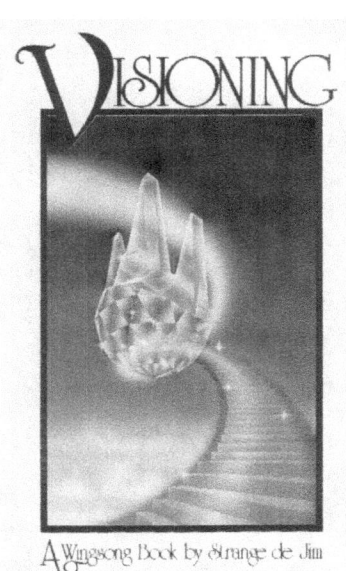

VISIONING

A Wingsong Book by Strange de Jim

now the whole book is available free to you, Dear Reader. Just go to page 132 for the details. How's that for magic?

Another part of Lisa's teachings involved contacting our wise old Spirit Guides. During one group session, I imagined a sort of Merlin/Gandalf/Yoda figure named Ash-Kar, who reached into his robe and handed me a business card reading: "Last Godking of Atlantis, Retired." I imagined him living in the park, a block from the Getty mansion at the end of Broadway, in San Francisco's exclusive Pacific Heights. So as not to block the magnificent view of San Francisco Bay, Ash-Kar's mansion was invisible, only flickering into view when guests were entering or leaving.

Lisa instructed us to ask for a gift from our Spirit Guides. We'd been assured we wouldn't have to share our secret wish with the group, so I figured I might as well just be honest:

STRANGE WISH #1
"I WANT TO MEET SOME MOVIE STARS!"

Next day a friend introduced me to his artist friend Satty, who invited me to a party at his studio in North Beach. When I arrived, film director Francis Ford Coppola (who knew me from Herb Caen's column) checked my name off the guest list. His presence, as you can imagine, was quite a surprise.

There were just two tiny rooms. But when I climbed down a ladder poking up through a trap door in the second one, I found lots of fun people in a large dirt-floored basement, which had been partitioned into a series of peculiar chambers.

I sat on a couch in the last of these rooms and wondered why I couldn't see my reflection in the mirror on the wall opposite. Had I turned into a vampire? Actually, the mirror was a framed hole in the wall, with the other room decorated exactly as a mirror image of the one I was in.

Just then a familiar-looking gentleman strode up to me, held out a genial hand and said, "Hi, I'm Jack Nicholson, and this is my pal, Michael Douglas." I was the only one present who had no idea this was the party for the San Francisco opening of *One Flew Over the Cuckoo's Nest*.

MY WISH HAD COME TRUE! I'd met my first movie stars! Color me stunned. I kicked myself for not having wished for something better. I certainly wanted to do more than just meet movie stars. After mulling it over, I asked Ash-Kar for a second wish. With a twinkle in his eyes Ash-Kar invited, "Be my guest."

STRANGE WISH #2
"I WANT TO BECOME THE WORLD'S GREATEST LOVER!"

Ash-Kar seemed delighted. He chuckled, "Good one, Strange!" and told me my wish was better than I knew. As for having it come true, he advised me to "work on it."

I Dream a Dream
About the Dreamer

That night I found myself meditating about Ash-Kar. I felt a twinge of guilt that I was using a Retired Godking as my own personal delivery boy and answer man. And here I'd been hogging all the attention in our imaginary conversations, never once bothering to ask what I might do for him. Where were my manners? Right before I fell asleep, I asked for more clarity about my genial old Spirit Guide. Did I ever get more than I bargained for!

In my dream, I was shown a vision of Atlantis a century before it sank beneath the waves. Ash-Kar, age 20, the newly ascended Godking, was entering Atlantis City's major temple. He was definitely younger, but I recognized him. Those eyes! That nose!

Ash-Kar was preparing to enter his first official Dream, to set the direction for his reign. As my own dream progressed, I found myself just knowing certain things about the scenes. No one was telling me anything; it was as if I had always been here.

On certain ritual occasions (and any time Atlantis was facing a major crisis), the Godking or Godqueen went into a ritual trance and Dreamed, and the Dream provided an Answer. The Godking would purify himself with several days of fasting and meditation. Then he would enter the Dream, merge into the Great Universal Currents, swimming around to find a Vision that would reveal the Cosmic view of what was going on in Atlantis and what, exactly, should be done about it.

Priest-scholars couldn't agree on whether the Dreamer left his body and traveled to real times and places, or whether the Dreams were entirely imaginary. But that was mere quibbling. The important thing was that at the beginning of his reign, and whenever necessary thereafter, the Godking Dreamed, and the Dream provided Answers.

In this, his first time out, Ash-Kar was attended by comely Jewel-Et and handsome Roh-Mio, who served as his Balancers.

Ash-Kar entered the pure white-marble pyramid perched atop the Temple's highest crystal tower. He lay on his back on the chamber's only furnishing, the white-marble slab which was located at the pyramid's precise focal point. Jewel-Et stood above his head and Roh-Mio at his feet. They would monitor him and balance the cosmic energy, the chi.

Ash-Kar Dreamed.

As Sirius B rose in the west, its light revealed a broad peaceful plain, dotted with large gray hippopotamus-like creatures munching on tasty lasha bushes. Sirius B's twin, Sirius A, hung in the southern sky, its light much fainter.

The hippo-esque creatures began to stir and yawn (as only hippo-esque creatures can). They'd neglected to develop large brains or opposable thumbs; so they were completely unable even to start a fire by rubbing two sticks together, much less farm, build houses, or invent such delights as nuclear weapons, digital watches or personal, user-friendly computers.

As a result, they had no jobs, no projects, no hobbies, no worthwhile endeavors on which they could lavish their time. Sad as it is to report, they were forced to spend their days wallowing around in mudholes and lumbering over the pleasant veldt, munching delicious lasha leaves.

They did have telepathy. Oh, nothing like you're thinking. They couldn't have conversations or anything like that. They weren't intellectual. They couldn't flash from mind to mind, "Ahem, did you hear the latest dirt on Bertha? Well, my dear, the way I heard it…"

Nothing like that. Not even thoughts, really.

Think of a flock of Earth birds all rising into the air at once and then wheeling and turning together. There was a sort of communication, a sort of communion below the level of thought. They mused together on the colors they saw (mostly green and blue and brown), the taste of lasha leaves, the smell of the veldt, the feel of mud and wind and rain, the sight of the giant red and green pyramids, and the sensations of mating. That was pretty much it.

All day and all night for thousands and thousands of years they mused together. Green and blue and brown, smell and taste and feel. Their musing was several notes blending into a single note. And that single note was Om.

Om.

Om.

For thousands of years.

Om.

Om.

Om.

The note sang out from the planet circling Sirius B, sang out into space, sang out into the Universe. Almost a beacon, really, for anyone able to sense it.

Ash-Kar followed the beacon, slipped into the body of a tiny-brained large-bodied hippo-esque creature named Horass, and found himself telepathically sharing pure sensations with his herd–the warmth of sunlight on hippo hide, the taste of delicious lasha leaves.

Then a peculiar thing began to happen. Faint pinkish and orangeish and blueish tints began to shimmer across hippo-esque epidermi. Strange bulges began to appear.

The colors became brighter and stronger, the bulges larger. Each hippo-esque being was designing his and/or her own color and shape *du jour*. Each hippo-esque creature began growing protuberances, and on the end of each protuberance was the most sensitive membrane in the Entire Known Universe (and parts of downtown Orion). And, when I say sensitive, I mean, don't even *think* too hard about them.

Horass chose a nice, roundish, paisley pattern, in mauve and chartreuse. When s/he considered s/himself a well-turned-out work of art, s/he began waddling around the plain. Horass was feeling amorous.

Actually all the hippo-esques were feeling amorous, and it didn't matter a single whit who paired up with whom. However, one liked to keep up appearances.

Eventually Horass found a nice contrasting partner, a shapely, squarish, hippo-esque lady (or possibly gentleman—it's hard to tell with shapes so very fluid), and the two set out to Lock Protuberances. The whole point of the daily exercise was to Lock Protuberances. You can't imagine how good Locking Protuberances felt.

But when you're dealing with erotic protuberances—especially when tipped with the most sensitive tissue in the Entire Known Universe (and parts of downtown Orion)—you don't just plop said membranes together. Horass and s/his partner waved protuberances at each other for a couple of hours, until they were so completely in tune they could finally, very, very carefully, very, very gently, touch the very tippy, tippy ends of their first pair of protuberances together.

The sensation! Oh, the sensation! Ash-Kar couldn't believe it. It made Atlantean sex (which, compared to other Earthling sex was pretty hot stuff) look like, well, pretty tame stuff.

Slowly, slowly, enjoying every second of the ritual, the partners increased the pressure until, finally, the first pair of protuberances was firmly locked together. Then they worked on the next pair. Eventually it turned out that Horass had two protuberances left over; so s/he hastily locked them together with a happy little sigh.

Now it was time for the main event. When all protuberances were firmly locked, Horass and s/his partner shut their eyes, embraced everything and *squeezed*. It wasn't so much a physical squeezing as just shutting your eyes and squeezing *everything*. And then it happened. Horass felt a couple mating…two couples mating, eight couples mating, everyone mating…AYEEYAH! The souls or essences of Horass and s/his partner squirted out of their bodies and joined the great Cloud of Pure Bliss which was forming above the planet.

The next four hours and fifty-three minutes were Pure Heaven. Horass and his planetmates were stripped to their naked essences, and all those naked essences were committed solely to Love. In fact, each pair of partners had reached inside, until they'd found and squirted out their real true essences, which *were* Love.

And when the rest of the hippo-esque creatures began slipping back into their bodies on Paradise, Ash-Kar slipped, instead, all the way back to his human body in Atlantis.

When Ash-Kar awoke back in Atlantis he had his subjects scatter to their bedchambers. As they lay with their communications crystals pressed to their energy centers, he sent them the essence of his Dream. Atlantis had its first continent-wide orgasm. Others followed monthly, at every full moon. For one hundred years.

There are the Puny Forces–fire, electricity, earthquakes, typhoons, volcanoes, etc. Then comes atomic fission. Then, atomic fusion. Then there's the Sex Drive.

The Atlanteans learned to harness their group sexual energy to make their wishes come true. Ash-Kar found that if they held images of what they wanted firmly in their minds, they could then actually use the group climaxes to bring about better social situations or even create physical objects. It was pure magic.

Alarmists had warned Ash-Kar and the Atlanteans that they might be disturbing more than just the surface of the earth with their magical climaxes, but they'd been enjoying them happily for years with no untoward results. To commemorate the 100th year of Ash-Kar's reign, the whole Continent had linked to build the largest Palace/Temple ever, and really poured their hearts and souls into it.

Oops! The alarmists had been right. All this intensely focused sexual energy had finally excited Earth to Her very core. Very early this morning the whole place had suddenly started to shake. And according to those who'd hastily studied the matter, this afternoon was going to be the Big One, and they'd better do something quick. It was Ash-Kar's responsibility to Dream up the solution.

Ash-Kar was at the Temple preparing. There'd been no time, of course, for the customary three-day fast. The best he'd been able to do was skip breakfast. He'd hastily bathed, and washed his long white hair and beard. He'd sped through a teensy bit of meditation. Now it was time. He could see by the colors in their auras that his attendants were exceedingly nervous.

Ash-Kar tried not to be anxious himself, but Catastrophe was staring him in the face, and he hadn't had time for adequate preparation. If he failed, all his people would die.

He couldn't think about that. He had to remain calm. He had to. Ash-Kar closed his eyes. He breathed deeply and cleared his mind. When all inside was quiet and still, he began reaching out, searching for the Great Shimmering Currents. Ah, it was beginning to work. Ah, he was entering the Dream, lifting out of his body…

Ash-Kar zoomed thousands of years into the future–into our own time, in fact–where he was attracted by the fifteen minutes of pleasure-pink and royal-purple flashes that accompanied my conception. He followed my career from afar until he was given the perfect chance to jump in as my "Spirit Guide."

Observing me giving massages, Ash-Kar finally sensed something in addition to the pure sexual energy the Atlanteans had been using–a loving, healing energy. But in Atlantis healing with sex was taboo! Ash-Kar slipped into a higher dimension to ponder, OM…

While he was OM-ing in the Strange world of his Dream, I woke up in my bed in San Francisco with my whole body humming in a most deliciously hippo-esque way.

I Study the Art of Swirling Chakras

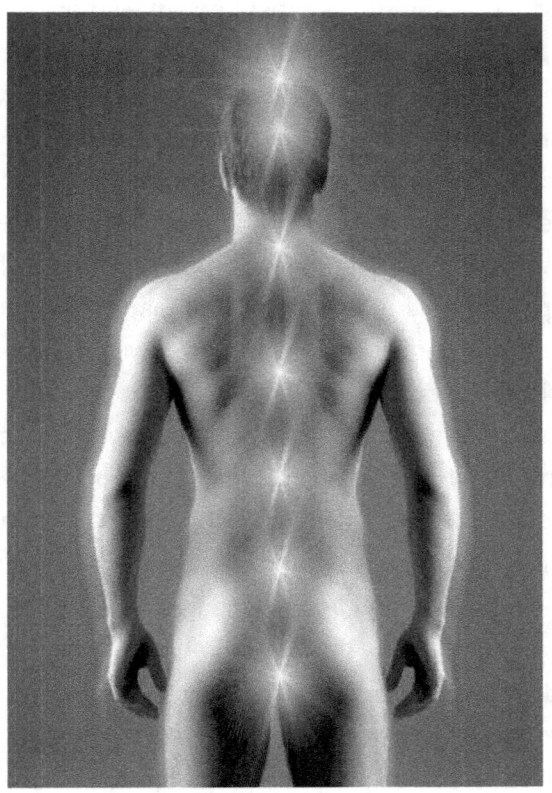

Deep within your being there exist
secret pleasure centers that have never known
the touch of human hands...
(Frontispiece of The Strange Experience)

When, at Lisa's invitation, I began investigating chakras, the first thing that struck me was how widespread these critters were. From the beginning of time, priests, magicians and healers in practically every culture have drawn pictures of the body with these same seven points of light.

Practices differ. Many Oriental healers, for example, believe the energy from the chakras is distributed through the body over the acupuncture meridians. Some Australian Aboriginals, on the other hand, think the energy circulates through the bloodstream, so all their rituals involve blood-letting. Other groups have other theories and, thus, other practices.

Deciding to try it myself, I began holding my hands over pairs of chakras during each massage. Often I couldn't feel anything at the beginning of a massage, but after we'd gotten in tune, I could definitely sense heat and some sort of electrical surge emanating from these seven magic locations. The necessary condition for producing these effects seemed to be my partner and me trusting each other, breathing deeply and evenly, and becoming very relaxed.

People would occasionally start raving about how they'd gone "somewhere else," somewhere "really out there," as I was puttering with their power points. Some would claim to have "lived" vivid scenes, either as pure hallucinations, or visits to past lives or other dimensions. And while they were doing that, I'd feel something too—not a scene, but a surge of energy and pure pleasure. The best times were when my partners would twitch as though they were getting delicious electric shocks. And on those happy occasions when the tingly portions were included, they were likely to experience what I came to think of as "shimmering orgasms," wondrous experiences that left both of us fascinated and delighted.

I got to experience the power of energy work on my own chakras when I began trading sessions with a gorgeous, quirky, amazing healer named Cary. I'd give him my regular combination of physical massage and energy balancing (concentrating, at his request, on the "weenie chakra").

The sessions he gave me were pure energy work. I'd lie on my back on his massage table, still wearing sweat pants and t-shirt. He'd simply touch two points on my body and breathe energy between them, touch two other points and breathe, etc. The effect was amazing. Afterwards the whole world would seem brighter and fresher and friendlier. I'd float around in a crystal-clear happy daze.

My massagees had told me about such things happening when I worked on them. Now I got to feel it for myself and know for sure that it was real. I could see that doing energy work well, and combining it with a physical massage, would pretty much be Heaven on Earth.

I continued massaging several new volunteers every week and watching what happened. All the sessions were enjoyable, but what especially interested me was that one massage in a hundred that was truly spectacular—where my partner's primary male organ (penis or clitoris) would become refreshingly engorged to the point where a little tug on this pubic hair, or even a little pinch on that toe or poke on this knee, would cause it to twitch; where available female organs would be blowing kisses, yelling, "Yoo hoo!" and drawing me in like industrial-strength whirlpools; and where the session would end in a shimmering climax.

Usually it had never happened to them before, so they'd think it was all my doing. I knew it only happened with one person in a hundred, so I knew it was them. But what was it about them? After a while, I realized it was their general attitude of appreciation and consideration toward everyone. In simple terms, these were people who, if they didn't want to have sex, would say, "I'm honored, but no thank you," rather than, "Yuck, you're disgusting." And if they did want to, they wouldn't try to trick or pressure or force the other party into it. They had a general attitude of appreciation, of opening—not just to me, but to all people, to the miracle of life itself.

Basically, it seems the more we humans overcome our internal ageism, racism, sexism and homophobia, drilled into us from birth, the more freely pleasure and healing can flow through our entire bodies, souls and dreams.

When I'd gone to massage school, I'd been first in the class in anatomy, learning the names of all the muscles and where they attached, etc. On Ash-Kar's advice, I resolved to forget this approach—forget even the names of the muscles—and learn to feel what was present right under my fingers.

So I jumped off the proverbial cliff and into the intuitive world, quitting my middle management job at Bank of America and moving to the Castro, San Francisco's major gay district. It was in that magical mecca that I tripped upon the next square in my all-too-checkered life...

I Stumble into
The Strange Experiences

One summer afternoon, at another New Age workshop, I'd been given a trust walk. My partner had blindfolded me and gently guided me around, keeping me from harm while leading me to fragrant flowers, smooth-barked trees, soft grass, cool water. It got a little scarier when we crossed a busy street; I could hear but not see the whizzing cars go by. I learned interesting things about trust, about how much I depended on sight, and about the possibilities of my other neglected senses.

Lady Jane Montgomery

The next night I was wearing my pillowcase to an opening of the theatrical version of *The Rocky Horror Picture Show* at the Montgomery Playhouse. My friend Lady Jane Montgomery, the proprietress, introduced me to actor/model **Cal Culver** (below), the lover of Tom Tryon, Hollywood movie star and best-selling author. Cal was intrigued by my pillowcased persona, and when I was telling Lady Jane about my trust walk, Cal immediately piped up, "I want one!"

So the next afternoon I was leading Cal around my neighborhood blindfolded when inspiration struck. I led him, still blindfolded, back to my apartment, placed his hands on my massage table and requested that he take off his clothes and climb aboard.

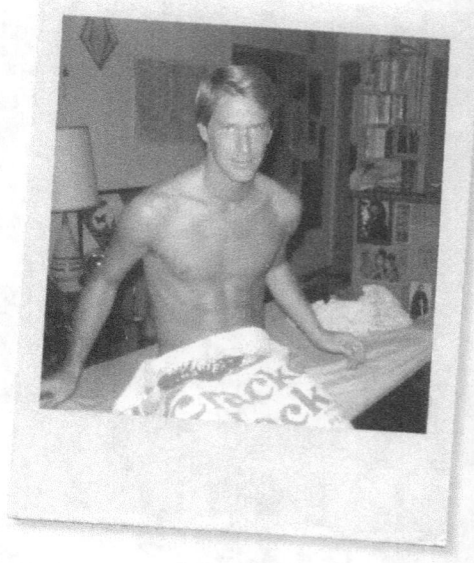

Afterwards he was all excited. "That was great!" he enthused. "I just wish I hadn't known it was you."

Perhaps he noticed my anguished expression, for he hastily added, "No, no. I just meant being blindfolded made me think how great it would be to get a massage from a pair of

The Count and Countess von Bergdorf shown here holding my friend Jake, who's wearing my pillowcase (don't ask).

strange hands–no, no, I mean from someone I'd never seen. Mystery really generates energy."

Thus was invented the "Strange Experience."

Cal blindfolded Lady Jane and drove her to my place for the second Experience, in which I didn't speak. Afterwards she was startled to take off her blindfold and discover yours truly.

Cal and Jane brought me a blindfolded **Bob Dulaney** (right), who played Rocky in *The Rocky Horror Picture Show*. Then they brought me a blindfolded Count and Countess von Bergdorf, and so it went.

The mood during the Experiences was very light. And whenever something funny happened I'd quit massaging for a few minutes while I wrote it down. Here are some of the conversations I had:

EXPERIENCEE (trying to ask whether to undress completely): "Uh, what about my genitals?"
ME: "Oh, just leave them on."

E: "I think I'm having a heart attack."
ME (performing a successful healing): "Well. Stop it!"

E: "Is my body supposed to be doing that?"
ME (showing my true ability as a healer): "Uh oh!"

ME: "Who are you imagining?"
E: "A tall green-eyed redheaded lady with big boobs."
ME: "This is going to be my most difficult Experience yet."

E: "Uh, could I ask what your, uh, sexual preference is?"
ME: "Sure. I just wait until I hear myself thinking, 'Good grief, what've I let myself get turned on by this time?'"

E: "What's your best opening line?"
ME: "'You're *really* beautiful!' usually does it, as long as it's delivered without too much conviction."

E: "You've done this with over three hundred people? What's wrong with a simple, 'Hi, let's be friends?'"
ME: "Would you have fallen for it?"
E: "Oh, I see what you mean."

E: "Well, I didn't know what a Strange Experience was, but I figured it was better than cleaning my kitchen. Which, incidentally, I still have to do."

E: "What if I get a stiffie?"
ME: "In that case I'll take out my butcher knife and cut..."
E: "Gasp!"
ME: "...another notch in the leg of my massage table."

ME: "If you had the World's Greatest Masseur at your disposal for the next few minutes, what part of your body would you have him work on?"
E: "My shoulders."
ME: "And how would you be lying?"
E: "Through my teeth."

People who'd had Strange Experiences would invite me to movies and parties. They'd ask if they could send their girlfriends and boyfriends for Experiences. Many of them liked to lounge around my apartment naked. Many of them would be so affectionate in public that people would ask if we were lovers. It was unbelievable that this was happening to me. What in the world was I doing during these massages that made all these people want to publicly and privately be such warm friends?

The secret is right there in the photo release that everyone signed when I wrote *The Strange Experience* (Ash-Kar Press, 1980). They said I could tell the public they'd enjoyed: 1) showing up blindfolded at the door of someone named Strange, 2) being invited to undress, and 3) being given a Strange massage with *no sex or violence no matter how hard they begged.*

Remember how I usually tried to have sex with the people I massaged? In the Strange Experiences I accidentally changed my strategy.

Here's why. These new blindfolded Experiencees hadn't seen me. They'd been sent by someone gorgeous, and might be expecting me to be gorgeous too. So even if they wanted me to include their heavenly portions during the massage, when they caught their first sight of me afterwards, they might go, "Yuck!" and complain to the friend who'd sent them. So even if they became aroused and were willing, I didn't dare include their best parts. They might have been a little hurt that I hadn't tried, but by not trying, I was perceived as *amazingly* trustworthy.

They didn't know why I hadn't tried to have sex with them. All they knew was that I was openly attracted to them, but hadn't taken advantage of them, even when they were literally naked (and for some of them, very willing). No stranger had ever given them a free massage or been in such an intimate situation and not even tried to have sex with them.

Trust attracts as strongly on the social plane as gravity does on the physical. Voila, we were instant best friends. Knowing you can trust someone with your naked body is very real and very primal.

Even if you can't touch their tingly portions, having gorgeous naked people curled around you is flat-out wonderful. And I learned another exceedingly valuable fact. People who can trust you with their tingly portions tend to. On second and later massages, now that they knew I could be trusted to *exclude* them, I was often given permission to *include* their tingly portions. Some even wanted to include mine. Some even wanted to date me. My love life turned platinum.

The same principle applies to other areas of life. You can be trustworthy with peoples' money, their secrets, their reputations, their homes, anything they value, with astonishing results.

Should you try being more trustworthy? That's up to you.

All I know is that when I tried it, I ended up just rolling in wonderful friends.

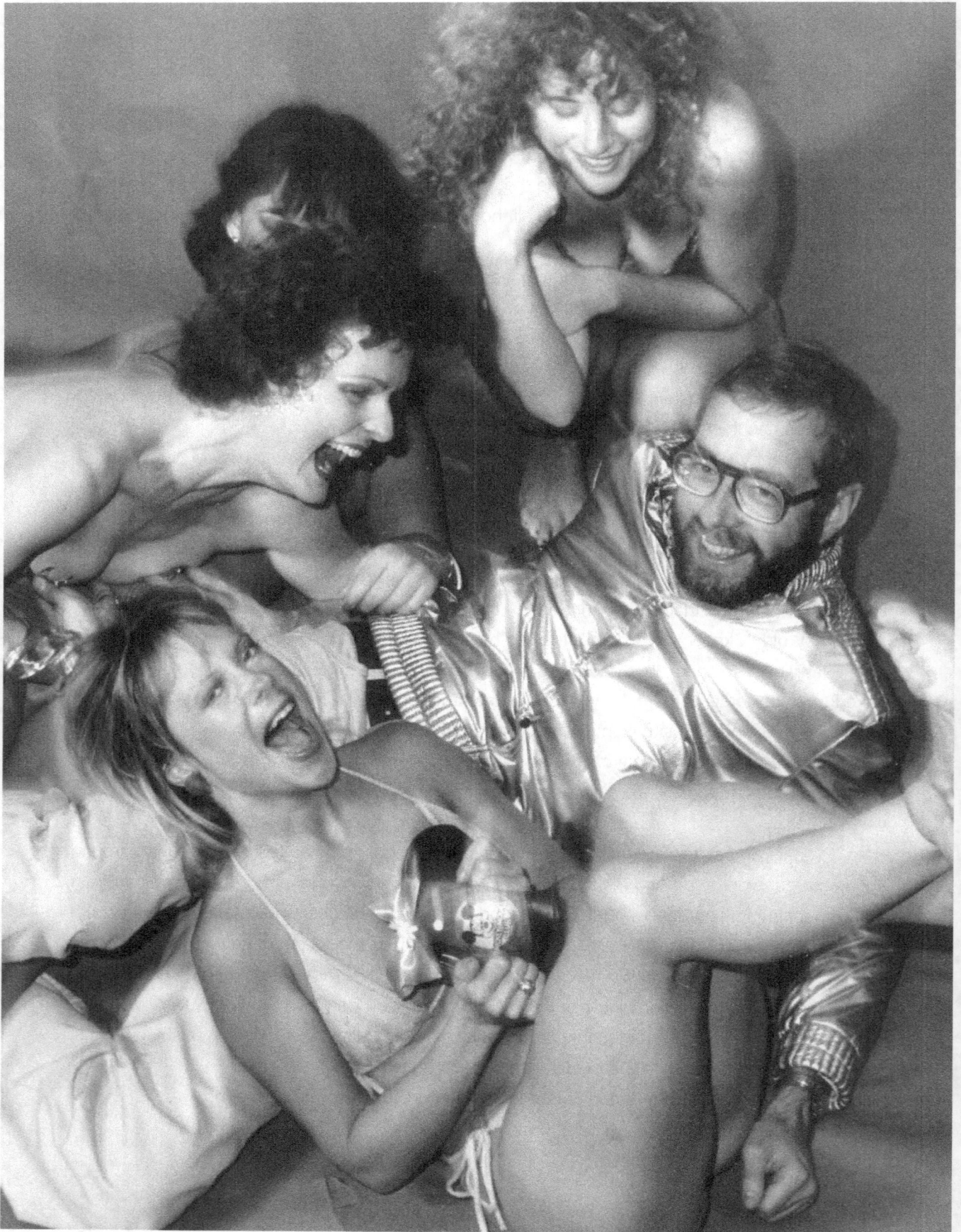

Andy Warhol Tells Me
A Strange Story

One evening Cal Culver called to ask if he could bring an Experiencee. He brought me an actual blindfolded Andy Warhol! And Andy loved the Experience so much he flew me back to New York with him.

On the plane he told me how he ended up gay. Right after high school he'd happily donated his virginity to an attractive thirty-something art collector. Having given Andy his first tour down under, she then treated him to a tour Down Under, flying him to Australia with her to look at Aboriginal art. One afternoon, while Andy's patroness was back in the hotel suite inspecting ancient artifacts stolen from sacred sites, Andy set off for Melbourne's famed Botanical Gardens to sketch the flowers (and, hopefully, meet a girl nearer his own age). Be careful what you wish. A giant 12-year-old young lady literally picked him up, threw him over her shoulder, and carried him into the bushes for precisely fifteen minutes of no-holes-barred carnal wrestling, with pink and purple flashes that were picked up by psychics around the globe. Andy became so frightened by young Edna's voracious va-jay-jay that he instantly fled from women to men. But he was even too traumatized to touch the men he now desired. He never had sex again, period. Needless to say, I had no idea this story had anything to do with me.

I Become a Man of the People

When I returned from New York I asked Ash-Kar for a hint on how I could become the World's Greatest Lover. He suggested I quit concentrating on cuties and celebrities, so I began massaging what eventually became thousands of naked men and women, twenty-something to elderly, all sizes, shapes, colors and persuasions. Some of them wanted the massages to have happy endings. If I was attracted, I was delighted to oblige. If not, I said I wasn't that kind of masseur. The latter left feeling rejected and unsatisfied, and I wasn't too happy either.

Finally I tried some unappealing tingly portions, and they weren't bad. In fact, they were fun. Then I tried a few more, and I found something I just never would have believed. It's enjoyable and entertaining and loving to help anyone climb to glory. We're all just folks, and on all of us the tingly portions are the best part. I found myself actually enjoying weekly mutual happy endings with a peppy senior citizen. You can't believe how freeing acceptance is, and the immense power to which it opens you.

I tried to envision a society in which we found everyone's tingly portions wonderful, rather than loving a few and rejecting most others. I wished such a free way of living wasn't just an impossible dream, and that everyone in the world could enjoy acceptance and respect. I wrestled with the problem through the early 1980s, and then I petitioned Ash-Kar.

I'd just given one of the most wonderful massages of my long and checkered career, with energy flowing freely and cleanly. Afterwards I was lying on my futon in a happy daze and decided to ask Ash-Kar for another wish to express both the still-star-struck me and the do-gooder:

STRANGE WISH #3
"I WANT TO FILL MY BED WITH MOVIE STARS
AND BRING ABOUT WORLD PEACE!"

Again, Ash-Kar seemed amused and pleased. "This will come in a way you'd never expect," he told me.

Tragedy Strikes

AIDS struck the Castro, and by the end of the decade, half my friends had died. I massaged both sick friends and strangers near death, and it was heart wrenching and frustrating. I could give them a little comfort, but couldn't make them well.

One thing that surprised me was that quite a few of these massagees really, really, really wanted their tingly portions included. In an institutional setting I'd have to say no, but in their homes I'd oblige them, and they were truly grateful. They didn't feel like such lepers anymore; simple love and pleasure were within their reach. I'll never forget one man the day before he died. He was very frail, but completely present and clear. He'd said goodbye to this world and was looking toward the Great Adventure, the great leap into the Unknown. Inspired by his example, I began to fear death less myself.

By the end of the decade things had started getting better. Enter a new, extremely cheery best friend.

There Is Nothing Like a Dame...
Edna!

In 1990 I caught Dame Edna Everage on *The Tonight Show*, and she had me laughing so hard I nearly fell off my futon. Then the local PBS station began running *The Dame Edna Experience*, the number one show in Britain, and I loved it too. But even that didn't prepare me for Dame Edna's autobiography *My Gorgeous Life*. I was captivated by the story of this ordinary Aussie housewife whose one-woman shows of humorous "sharing and caring" had propelled her to

Megastardom, giving her the means to do good through her charity organizations, Endnacare Switzerland and (because of hubby Norm's plumbing problem) The Dame Edna Prostate Foundation.

I was first in line when Dame Edna came to San Francisco on her international book tour. Something electric happened the instant she squeezed my hand. In her book she'd said, "Don't run away with the idea that I can heal. What a vain woman I would be if I set myself up as a one-woman Lourdes! But spooky things have happened during my performances, and barely a night goes by after one of my shows when the cleaners do not discover, in the aisle or under a seat, a pair of crutches, a Zimmer frame or a prosthetic device. I make no greater claim than that." I can testify her mere touch made me feel better.

When I gushed about how her life story had inspired me, Dame Edna invited me back to her hotel suite. There she introduced me to her manager Barry Humphries and told him, "I had the most peculiar feeling when I met Strange. It was as though we'd known each other for years." I was pleased as punch, and admitted I'd felt an immediate kinship with her too.

She was gracious enough to give me her London number so I could call when I needed no-nonsense-yet-caring advice. I'm not ashamed to say I consulted her a number of times when I was hesitant to bother Ash-Kar, and even with her grueling schedule, Dame Edna was never too busy to give me excellent advice. "Listen to your heart, Strange, Possums," she'd tell me. "Listen to your heart."

For the rest of the 1990s and early 2000s I was pleased that society was becoming much more accepting of gay people. Perhaps we could all learn to get along after all, a lesson some of our closest animal cousins had already mastered. I was given more hope for humans when I learned about the bonobo, the "make love not war" apes with whom we share over 95% of our DNA. When the bonobo spot food, for instance, instead of fighting over it, they enjoy sexual foreplay first, and then loll around sharing the goodies. All the adults are bisexual, and they all have friendly, comfy sex with each other (except parents with their own offspring). Perhaps humans could adopt some of their ways. That's how far I'd gotten in my quest for World Peace when I was suddenly kidnapped.

The Baroness Ethelina von Elm
I Meet The Magic Nipples

One afternoon a year ago I answered the doorbell to find Robin Williams, of all people, on my doorstep. I'd met him several times, and we'd both delivered eulogies at columnist Herb Caen's funeral in 1997, but I couldn't imagine how he even knew where I lived. His words didn't clear up the mystery. "Pack an overnight bag and hop in the limo, Strange. You've just hit the jackpot! Somebody wants to meet you."

"Who?"

"You'll see."

Robin had been sworn to secrecy and wouldn't even give me a hint as we drove to the airport, flew on a private jet to L.A., then limo-ed to Beverly Hills. When we pulled up in front of the famous mansion of the woman who'd recently bought the E! network I knew who we were going to see.

As I stepped out of the car I saw a mass of pleasure-pink hair, heard a bellowed, "Strange, Cowpossums!" and was clasped to the world's most famous bosom. Snuggling into my armpits were the magic nipples that had launched a thousand unions. Sandwiched between them, my chakras were buzzing up a perfect storm.

Now, for those of you who don't know better, I'd like to straighten out the rather convoluted record. Baroness Ethel wasn't always the luxuriantly pink-haired socialite with the booming voice you may know from talk shows, E! and You-Tube clips. Now that I've gotten to know her, I'd like to share the true story of how she became a Baroness and the world's second-richest woman. It's quite a whopper!

The Baroness grew up simply as Ethel Mae Peabody in Lesser Tuna, Texas. At puberty, she shot up to six feet, with spectacular bosoms that would have been ample on someone twice her size. Soon after, she discovered that her nips had magical powers. One day at school, she experienced an amazing electric tickling at the tips of her chest, and suddenly felt compelled to shove two classmates into the janitor's closet and lock the door. By the time they were finally liberated, her geeky girlfriend and the football jock had become an inseparable twosome.

Four more times during her high school years, Ethel's nips tingled. Each time she impulsively performed some unusual action. Twice, two seemingly unsuited people found themselves in love. Once, her boyfriend was prevented from getting on a plane that crashed on takeoff, and once, well...

At the end of her senior year, jilted by her boyfriend, Ethel spent her prom night in a bar in neighboring Greater Tuna, where, in the midst of her depression, she was suddenly bucked up by the arrival of the most *fascinating* Frenchman. Ethel tingled as she had never tingled before. And Andre, helped along by Ethel's judicious applications of bourbon and branch, actually ended up springing for a trip to Paris!

She and her new Sweetie-Pie drove back to her place. Taking no chances, she stealthily crawled into her bedroom window, packed the odd necessity, left a brief (and somewhat evasive) note for her parents, and crawled back out the window. Thirteen hours later, she and Andre were whooping it up in Gay Paree.

Well, Andre turned out to be a louse, who a week later ran off to Florence with an art student of the same name. But, besides leaving Ethel cold, he also left her with her return plane ticket and enough money for another three or four days in the City of Light.

Ethel, however, wanted to shine longer; so she began ladylike inquiries concerning gainful employment. Her luck was in. That very evening found her bouncing across the stage of the Crazy Horse Saloon, good-naturedly trying to cover at least something with her feathers, while showing these American tourists and real-honest-to-God Frenchmen the moves that had made her the most popular majorette at Lesser Tuna High.

The crowd had never seen anything like Ethel. And at least one member found himself smitten. At his table down front, shortish, stoutish, twenty-one-year-old Baron-to-be Frederick von Elm suddenly found his heart pumping bullets.

Frederick was a demure lad, painfully aware of his short stature and excess poundage. He spent most of his youth puttering with his electronic and ham radio equipment. To be fair, he'd been given little chance to polish his social side. His father, the current Baron von Elm, was certainly the most proper (and reputedly the richest) man in Europe.

This was only the second time young Frederick had ever escaped the surveillance of Fritz ("The Leech"), his bodyguard. Frederick had hied immediately to the fleshpots. And now he was in love. The realization hit him like a bus. That scantily clad girl up there on the stage was so pretty, so vital, so alive. And her breasts were so BIG. It scared him, of course, but, *sacre bleu*, it thrilled him even more.

The shy Frederick had no idea that flowers or candy, sent to the dressing room, might magically produce Ethel at his table within, let's say, two minutes. He sat there for a good half-hour after Ethel had departed the stage, not about to leave, but also not having a clue as to how to go about meeting her.

Then he thought he spied Fritz on the other side of the room. Like a short startled rabbit,

Frederick bolted out the front door, where he collided with Ethel, who'd just had a couple of quick drinkie-winkies in the *artiste's* dressing room, and was setting out for the boulevards to see what the evening might bring.

"Oops! Careful there, cowboy!" Ethel cautioned, lending the tubby little squirt a friendly steadying arm. Feeling her nips tingle, she scanned her companion more closely. Now, Ethel was not yet, by anyone's standards, a True Woman of the World, but she could see from his clothes that Frederick was rich, and she could tell from the way he was goggling at her that he found her attractive. "Hmm," Ethel reasoned, and acted accordingly.

In short, before Frederick could bumble up an introduction, he'd already been bundled into a cab and was well on his way to showing Ethel a good time. The next morning he awoke in a luxury suite at The Ritz, with a head the size of his bedmate's native Texas, filled with the knowledge that at last, gulp, he and Ethel were no longer, gulp, gulp, virgins (well, she still *wasn't*, Ethel figured).

Before Frederick had awakened, Ethel had browsed absently through his wallet. His name hadn't meant anything to her, unfortunately, and he wasn't her usual athletic "type." She'd almost made the Blunder of the Century by letting him slip through her capable fingers unscathed. But the currency and other clues had convinced her he really was rich. And somehow he had managed to produce just the most amazing sensations all over her breasts and nips. And he was sort of cute, and he was a genuine European. Bottom line, Lesser Tuna, and especially her louse of a boyfriend, would just die. Frederick, after coffee had somewhat settled his stomach, found himself on the phone arranging a quickie marriage to the bedazzling (and forceful) girl of his dreams.

Fritz tracked down the honeymooners two days later, and Ethel soon found herself locked with her new hubby into the back of a limo, speeding inexorably toward her new father-in-law's estate. From Frederick's description it didn't strike her as a meeting she'd enjoy. However, since even furious thought produced no plan for escaping the efficient Fritz, Ethel's firm loyalty to her new mate did not (that all-important visibly, at least) waver.

Fritz had briefed the old Baron on Ethel's background and the conditions under which she'd snared his son. After greeting this Brazen Temptress coldly, the Baron drew Frederick aside to discuss the annulment. But, inspired by steadfast Ethel's brave example, the dreamy Frederick stood up to his father. He never had before. He never would again. No one was more surprised than Frederick himself. But he wouldn't give up the woman he loved. "Disinherit me if you will," he whimpered determinedly, "but she's the only wife for me." Frederick was an only child. The poor Baron really had no choice.

A year later the priggish old Baron slipped in the bathroom of his new mistress's apartment (Ethel had introduced them), hit his head on the washbasin, and drowned in the toilet. His mistress panicked and fled. The old Baron was discovered three days later by the concierge, smelling to high heaven (the old Baron, not so much the concierge) and dressed (again, the old Baron) in leather and fishnet attire in which he would *not* have wished to be caught dead. Young Frederick succeeded to the title, and Ethel became a Baroness!

The Baroness Ethelina von Elm promptly set out to conquer the world. With her talent and Fred's title (not to mention money), the sky could no longer be considered the limit.

For the next four decades Ethel dazzled the world with her extravagant parties and wild practical jokes. She'd mix royalty and megastars with common folks. "Half somebodies and half nobodies" was her favorite mix. You never knew whom you'd meet or what would happen at one of Ethel's famous "do's."

Her tingling nips matched up unlikely celebs from Sonny and Cher, right down to You-Know-Who and David Letterman. And her jokes! She tricked five-year-old Prince Andrew into slipping a whoopee cushion onto Queen Elizabeth's throne. And guess who depantsed the President of the United States on live tv? But you couldn't stay mad at Ethel, because her heart was as big as her native Texas. She never put on airs and was right there for every worthwhile charity. Everybody loved Ethel. But what could she possibly want with me?

I Receive the Shocking News

As soon as we'd been ushered into the mansion and served drinks and plates of goodies the Baroness asked Robin and me to sit down, and began a story she said would astonish us.

"A little over a year ago, Cowpossums, the woman I'd always believed to be my mother suffered a stroke, and of course, I immediately high-tailed it back to Lesser Tuna. On her deathbed Mom finally made a confession. She wasn't my mother at all! She claimed my real Mom was Filonia ("Fifi") Fulbright Bo-ku. And that's not all! Oh my dears, she claimed that somewhere Down Under, I had a twin sister named Edna Beazley!"

Shocking as it was, I couldn't understand why Robin and I were being told this story.

"Who's Edna Beazley?" I ventured. The name sounded familiar.

"Why, Dame Edna Everage!"

"Wow! She's one of my best friends!" I was still at a loss. "But why are you telling us all this?"

Baroness Ethel dropped into her Chippendale chair, which creaked ever so slightly. "One morning in the suburb of Moonee Ponds when Edna was 12, puberty finally hit her in her morning bath. Edna knew what was happening to her. She'd watched the kangaroos and the dingoes. And she'd been planning for years that her debut deflowering should be in Melbourne's famous Botanical Gardens."

Believe it or not, I still hadn't tumbled.

"There she was lured into the shrubbery by a visiting American artist, Andy Warhol. And YOU–" she pointed a seriously bejeweled finger at me, "you, Strange, are the fruit of that day in the bushes!"

She reached across the table to clutch me to her more-than-ample bosom. "COME TO AUNTIE ETHEL!" the Baroness bellowed in conclusion.

Dame Edna and Andy Warhol my parents?! It would explain everything! "I don't believe it!" I exclaimed.

My new Aunt Ethel had a report from a DNA expert which explained how he'd taken a generous stain on a little white towel, tastefully framed in the bedroom of Hollywood's hottest hunk, and compared it to a few pitiful beads of sweat on a silver wig in the Andy Warhol museum.

Then he'd compared those results to saliva I'd left on the cup after drinking my coffee one morning at San Francisco's Café Flore. There was no other conclusion. I was the lovechild of Andy Warhol and Dame Edna Everage.

I still didn't believe it, but Baroness Ethel showed me the transcript of an Australian court case in Moonee Ponds, the year I was born. The parents of a minor, a "Miss B," were suing the local doctor for the botched delivery of a male bubba named "Strange." They claimed the baby had been dropped on his soft spot. The doctor said the umbilicus had acted like what we today would call a bungee cord, and the baby's noggin never nicked the linoleum. The nurse, however, testified about the smell of spirits on the doctor's breath, and a suspicious wet spot on the floor, which the doctor had surreptitiously tried to cover with his foot. The fact that the judge refused to strike the words "suspicious" and "surreptitiously" shows where his sympathy lay. He found for the plaintiffs, and little Edna traipsed off to buy her first pair of spangled "Hollywood-style" spectacles. More investigation had revealed the Strange baby had been given up for adoption to an American couple from Charleston, WV. That seemed pretty conclusive. And dropped on my soft spot? That too would explain everything.

But wait a minute. This couldn't be true. For one thing, look at me, and look at my supposed parents. As you can see, there's absolutely no family resemblance. Besides, my younger brother, who I *know* came from my West Virginia mother, looks very much like me.

I know I should have said, "No, I can't possibly be your nephew," but if the Baroness Ethel believes you're her nephew, you're her nephew.

I was amazed that Aunt Ethel had read *Visioning* and *The Strange Experience* as part of her research on me. I was even more amazed to find that her detectives had stalked, er, talked to several of my friends. "I wanted to see how Strange a nephew I'd acquired, Cowpossums," she confided.

"Er, what does Dame Edna say about all this?" I asked.

"Well, why don't we ask her?" Aunt Ethel beamed. She hit a button, and there was Dame Edna on the big wall screen, live from London.

"Hello, Strange, Possums! Welcome to the family!" She was appearing in her new West End show, and couldn't get away, so, since Aunt Ethel had done all the detective work, she'd graciously let her break the news to me. (I flew to London two weeks later for a big happy family visit.)

Meanwhile, Aunt Ethel decided to install me in Guest Cottage #2, a large four-bedroom house with a butler to take care of all my needs. As we strolled over, I saw four movie stars already splashing in the pool. Luckily, my cottage windows looked right out over the shallow end. Aunt Ethel left me to settle in and told me to come to the mansion at eight for dinner.

When I ambled over, Aunt Ethel introduced me to Baron Frederick, my new Uncle Fred. We were exchanging the amiable if somewhat wary hellos of two nice fellows who are suddenly related, when Aunt Ethel boasted that Uncle Fred had developed an amazing new building

Me and my supposed parents—though I see no family resemblance whatsoever.

material called Lazaglass™, which made an entire structure a giant HDTV. Uncle Fred and Sweet Georgie Lucas were building, hush-hush, a showcase Crystal Palace on a hill overlooking Skywalker Ranch outside San Francisco.

For their upcoming fortieth wedding anniversary, Fred had decided to "say it with architecture." And my new uncle was a complete science and techno-whiz; not for nothing were his best friends Steven Hawking and Steve Jobs. He was presenting Ethel with a cross between the Taj Mahal and Cinderella's Castle, updated for the 21st century.

Aunt Ethel was already planning a huge 40th Anniversary Palace Warming. I just had to come.

That evening, Ethel showed me the plans for the Palace. Fred blushed as she gushed. The Grand Ballroom, with its circular white marble stage and 2000-guest capacity, was the perfect theater for an Event of the First Magnitude. What kind of entertainment could Auntie Ethel offer the guests? *Cirque du Soleil* to open, of course, and then the biggest musical artists in the world. But she needed a theme.

"Love," I suggested, not quite articulating the *duh*.

"Whatever do you mean?"

"I don't know. I'm just thinking out loud. It's your anniversary. Maybe passing on the lessons of love to the new generation...Wait a minute! How about Romeo and Juliet?"

"What?"

"You're famous for matchmaking. Pick the most wonderful young man and woman in the world and have them...have them meet for the first time onstage...like a modern Romeo and Juliet."

"Yes! Oh, I'm tingling!"

"Oh, but wait. What do we do with them after they've met?"

"Don't worry, Cowpossum. I know this is right. We'll figure out the details later."

It was crazy to go ahead on such a nebulous plan, and anyone but my new Aunt Ethel would have rejected it out of hand. Within seconds, shrewd visionary that she was, she was on her cell, IM'ing David Geffen, Steven Spielberg and Sweet Georgie to help her turn the Palace Warming into a major-motion-picture redo of *Romeo and Juliet* for the New Millenium. And the leads would be two unknowns, strangers to each other and the world. Mystery *does* generate energy! Within days, news would leak out all over the world.

"Oh my dear, I just *knew* you were family," was Aunt Ethel's parting remark, "and in the morning, if she's still alive, you can meet your real grandmother."

I was getting used to the idea that Auntie Ethel was family. In fact, I loved it. But after the few tidbits she'd told me about Fifi from the private detective reports, I was feeling understandably nervous about coming face to wrinkled face with the Mother of Us All.

Filonia ("Fifi") Fulbright Bo-Ku
Shaking off the Boston Blueballs

Boston, Eighty-odd Years Ago. "Filonia's such a *restless* child," Patience Fulbright would explain to her Boston Back Bay visitors. She'd watch *their* daughters demurely sipping tea at her mansion, while Filonia fidgeted, squirmed and, like as not, dashed from the room without remembering to be excused, probably lumbering into something breakable on the way out. "Special" children can be a trial to their parents, especially when they've inherited the peculiar traits these same parents have spent their whole lives denying in themselves.

Patience and Arnold Thornby Fulbright were blessed with world-class sex drives, and could have enjoyed a marriage that was a true paradise of sensual delight. Instead, they were each so embarrassed about being so oversexed that they didn't want anyone to know, especially not each other. As a result their lovemaking was so prim and proper and awkward that by mutual unspoken consent they didn't resume their sex life after their first and only child's birth. As a rule, Patience and A. Thornby Fulbright *vibrated*, rather like soundly struck tuning forks.

One afternoon when she was eight, Fifi and the little servant boy Rupert had sneaked off by themselves into the pantry to play doctor. As soon as Fifi had touched Rupert's little nubbin, she'd felt like the young Mozart, running his fingers for the first time over the keys of a harpsichord or virginal. Yes! Fifi had found her Calling. She was going to be a Healer, and she was going to specialize in wee-wees. No longer an outcast! Everything made sense; she'd found her niche. Oh, Fifi felt so wonderful!

And then suddenly her mother was in the doorway shrieking, "YOU HORRID CHILD!" Patience was beside herself. It was bad enough that Filonia wasn't pretty. But this!

For her part, the instant her mother's screech penetrated her unattractively outsize ears, young Fifi let go of little Rupert's wee-wee and promptly peed herself.

It was a classic confrontation. Small children the world over grasp instinctively the relationship between Healing and Sex. The game of Doctor is played the same everywhere. To heal people you have them remove their garments, and then you run your hands delightedly over their nude bodies, accepting and cherishing each and every part along the way.

All over the world since the beginning of time children have known this, and nearly all over the world since the beginning of time parents have assured their offspring they were very much mistaken. And few parents have ever assured them with quite the verve, quite the note of repulsion and horror, as Patience Fulbright the afternoon she caught her "difficult" daughter inspecting the, ugh, "thingie," of the butler's young son. (The fact that young Rupert looked much more like her husband than like the butler may have had something to do with Patience's reaction.)

With her sexuality decidedly squashed, Fifi's pent-up frustration led her into making all sorts of mischief. There was the ferret loosed at a Vanderbilt wedding, the serpent in the coffin at a Cabot funeral. Ten years later, Fifi's escalating scandals brought even her father to his knees. That nasty article on the front page of the *Boston Globe* was the final straw.

Arnold Thornby Fulbright was not a man to spoil even his favorite (all right, only) daughter with "crass material gifts." Yet now, so anxious was he to remove Fifi (and the dust she'd kicked up) from society's irritated eye that he insisted on springing for a round-the-world luxury cruise. Not only that, he actually pretended to swallow the absurd proposition that adequate chaperonage for the sprightly Fifi could be provided by his dithering unmarried sister Rebecca.

Fifi liked the idea of the cruise, and that night she had a dream that on her trip she would find a royal mate. Before her pater could change his mind, Fifi set sail to find her Prince.

Fifi could soon be spied batting her cheerful (if not especially lovely) lashes at a handsome ship's officer, while Aunt Becky rummaged in her carryall for her knitting. There was Fifi, at an outdoor cafe on the Champs-Elysees, wriggling her skinny nose at a passing French Count, while Aunt Becky gushed innocently to a notorious international confidence man that she never expected to find *herself*, of all people, sipping an "actual alcoholic beverage" in such charming company. Why, there was Fifi on Rome's Via Venito, subtly wagging her fun-filled (though angular) hips at a pair of giggling Italian sailors, as she pointed out to Aunt Becky the fascinating religious artifacts displayed in the handiest shop window. And, good gracious, that was young Fifi wiggling her large talented ears at a startled Arabian Emir as the ship passed through the Suez Canal.

Fifi was cutting, as the poet says, a swath. And she kept feeling she was drawing closer and closer to her Prince Charming. As the ship neared India, this intuition became positively intense. Oh, where would he be? What would he be like? She just bet he was a dashing young titled British officer.

The last night before landfall, Fifi had a compelling dream. She saw herself as a Princess among adoring brown-skinned subjects. Could her true love possibly be a genuine romantic young Indian Prince? She was sure that was it. She was quite wrong.

At this stage in Fifi's spiritual development, she can perhaps be forgiven for never even dreaming her Prince Charming would actually turn out to be a seventy-two-year-old Calcutta "street masseur" with only the sketchiest notions of personal hygiene. But shouldn't she at least have recognized him when she literally stumbled across him in the street? No matter. Bo-ku recognized her the minute she came tripping around the corner from Government House.

"Hairy Krishna!" Bo-ku cried. Here was the soul-mate with whom he'd shared so many action-packed incarnations. Here was the one being in all the Universe whose "vibratory rate" was exactly equal to his own. It was his Beloved. Before Fifi could even summon up international sign language for, "Yuck! No thank you!" she found Bo-ku had "warmed her chakras" and slid her smoothly through The Unmarked Door to Paradise. Fifi had no idea what was happening to her. She hadn't even known she possessed chakras. She'd certainly never had her chakras warmed.

Right there in the crowded street, Fifi felt herself begin to glow inside. Really, it was the most marvelous feeling. When Bo-ku (who, luckily, spoke English, though with a heavy British accent) explained they were soul-mates, Fifi's mind rejected the idea completely. But her heart and soul believed him implicitly. She knew Bo-ku spoke truth when he claimed they'd been lovers forever.

Right there on the pavement he had her close her eyes, and he showed her the most marvelous things. He touched just the top of her head and the middle of her forehead, and she caught glimpses of–well, "higher things" is the only way she could put it. And Bo-ku began to seem, not just young and handsome, but positively godlike. She found that she could think of nothing better than living with Bo-ku, learning from him and loving him. She found herself, in short, agreeing to marry him.

FiFi's Brief, Exceedingly Eventful Marriage

It was a staggered Aunt Becky who, to avert the even larger catastrophe of having her niece "live in sin among the savages," served as bridal attendant in a "devil-inspired ceremony" the next morning. The poor lady, as she kept muttering over and over, didn't know what she was going to tell her brother and sister-in-law back in Boston. She solved the problem by disappearing for the rest of her formerly natural life into the Anglican mission in Bombay.

As the pinch-faced minister at the hastily thrown-together Episcopalian ceremony had announced (in a cracked voice), "You may, hack, choke, kiss the bride," Bo-ku had planted a chaste kiss on Fifi's right ear and whispered, "Come, thou April moon, serenely shining o'er my long December nights."

Well, what would you have done, Dear Reader? It was just the sort of poetic invitation Fifi had always imagined her Prince Charming would issue; so, of course, she'd accepted at once. Now, two hours later, Fifi was outside Calcutta, in the suburbs. Smelling of jasmine, dressed in a fresh white 100%-cotton sari, garlands of flowers draped around her neck, a little dab of red paint daubed into the middle of her forehead, Fifi was sitting cross-legged beside Bo-ku on a raised dais. She was being married again, and this time in a ceremony that wasn't awkward and perfunctory.

Bo-ku's family, his few hundred closest disciples, were now squatting on the ground staring raptly at her. They were behaving quite well compared to Aunt Becky, but there was no concealing the fact they were all agog at the realization that their revered spiritual grandfather had just picked up in the street a tall, awkward, eighteen-year-old Occidental bride.

Fifi's favorite secret color had always been Limelight; so, to tell the truth, she was loving all the attention. She'd married what she'd thought was a poor beggar, and he'd turned out to be a popular guru. She really was going to be a Princess in an exotic foreign land!

But things weren't quite that simple. On one hand she was the Beloved Wife of the Guru, the ashram's number two personage. But she was also the most backward student in the whole establishment. She didn't know anything about anything–the customs, the beliefs, the language. It was very confusing being treated as half-queen, half-idiot.

Two weeks after her wedding it all came to a head. Bo asked the unthinkable of her. "Come," he said, and led her out of the ashram to a little clearing close to a burbling stream. They sat down cross-legged. Bo seemed to be waiting for something.

An elderly and rather reeking gentleman hobbled over. A filthy rag constituted his sole article of clothing. Gingerly, trying to position himself so he wouldn't put pressure on any of his three open running sores, he eased himself to the ground.

Fifi felt her gorge rising. "Oh, please," she prayed–whether to her Episcopal God or some of the Hindu ones she wasn't sure–"please don't let me disgrace myself." Maybe if she closed her eyes. But, oh, the smell! She was going to be sick. No, she could make it. She could sit here while Bo did whatever he was going to do. Wait, Bo was saying something to her. With great effort she opened her eyes and, avoiding their new companion, looked at Bo. Bo said, "Let us massage him."

"No!" Fifi shrieked. She leapt to her feet and was just able to make it to the stream before getting sick. Then she collapsed, sobbing, under a banyan tree. Bo sat down beside her.

"I can't live here!" Fifi wailed. "I've tried, but I can't! I'll never get used to it! Oh, please, let me go back to Boston!"

"Yes, too many new things at once," Bo said. "Of course, you may go back to Boston if you wish." He thought a minute. "But if you'd be willing, I'd like to take you someplace very quiet first, a place where you can think and decide what you really want to do."

"All right," Fifi agreed. The quiet place turned out to be a little quieter and twenty thousand feet higher than she'd anticipated.

Bo-ku simply clasped Fifi's hands and had her close her eyes. When she opened them they were in Tibet, in Bo's hermit-style cave at 21,200 feet, a lone stick of sandalwood incense adding just that certain flavor and body to the thin, diamond-crisp Himalayan air. "Ah, it is a joy to share this with you," Bo smiled.

While the Alps prompt yodeling, the Himalayas prod one to mystical feelings. Fifi and Bo-ku contemplated the view in companionable silence for an hour or so. Then a comment–a question, really–welled up in Fifi's mind. Bo had just teleported them both hundreds of miles. She wanted to do magic, too.

"How can I develop my psychic powers?" Fifi mused, barely aloud. (Bo would be free to let the question float on by or to answer it, as he chose.)

"Is it proper for you at this time?" he replied. "Ask your intuition." Ask her psychic powers whether she should develop her psychic powers! How very like her adorable Bo.

"I feel...awkward in the ashram when everyone else can do things I can't," Fifi confessed. Really, in spite of all Bo's assurances that these magical abilities were really hindrances to Enlightenment, it was humiliating to sit there like a kindergartner while everyone else was astral projecting, walking on fire, sticking sharp pointy objects through themselves without screeching, floating in midair, materializing solid objects out of nothing, and whatnot.

"Awkwardness," Bo commented, "an interesting emotion. Much can be learned from awkwardness."

Fifi wasn't to be sidetracked. "I think I'm afraid of the powers," she persisted in confessing. "When I think of floating out of my body, for instance, I'm afraid of falling."

Fifi suddenly realized that in the highly touted "Here and Now" she was perched on the lip of a cave at 20,000 feet. Oops!

"Apt observation," Bo-ku commented. "May I suggest that you close your eyes and ask what your calling is, your purpose in life?"

Oh, poo, that was too big and vague. Fifi felt like rejecting the suggestion. But then she wasn't sure, and then she remembered what a rare opportunity this was for her to benefit from her unique position as Bo-ku's wife and favorite-though-least-advanced pupil. For, in spite of all the chelas (disciples) praying for his attention, Bo chose to devote a good deal of his time to her private instruction.

Her famous husband was sitting with his eyes rolled up into his head, enthusiastically chanting some ancient Tibetan ditty which just sent shivers up Fifi's spine.

Bo. Wait. He'd given her some advice. Oh no, she'd completely forgotten what it was. It was one of those assignments, too, where if you carried it out, you just learned gobs and gobs.

All right. It was in her mind. She just had to dredge it up. They'd been sitting here, and she'd been fretting about her lack of psychic powers, and Bo had said...Bo had said...Come on now, Bo had said–SHE SHOULD MEDITATE ON HER PURPOSE IN LIFE!

"Of course!" Fifi thought. "If I know where I'm going, I'll know whether developing psychic powers would help me get there. And I'll know which psychic powers to develop. Bo is just the cat's pajamas!"

Fifi shut her eyes and began the breathing exercises. She used the spiral pattern for opening her chakras. Her purpose in life. Her purpose in life. What was her purpose in life? Nothing.

Then, inside her head, she heard Bo suggest, "Ask your future self." Fifi tried to picture herself older and wiser.

"How old?" she wondered.

Bo-ku seemed amused. "Eighty-five," he suggested.

Eighty-five!" Fifi thought. "Am I going to live that long?" That was certainly reassuring.

Fifi tried to imagine herself as an old woman, reach out to that older Fifi. Suddenly she felt her insides beginning to glow. Oh, it was happening! She was going to astral project! She felt herself floating out of her body on a long silver cord. Ah, she was riding on Bo's haunting chant, soaring up over the highest peaks and down into a secret peaceful hidden valley, riotous with flowers, known in legend as Shangri-la.

Fifi landed safely on the shore of a lake beside a lovely rainbow staircase. She began climbing until she'd spiraled up to a miniature Crystal Palace hanging in the sky. She stepped through the doorway and found herself dazzled. She was in a futuristic ballroom crowded with scandalous party-goers. And there, on the stage, was a burly elderly woman in a low-cut crimson gown and bright purple hair. Oh no! It was herself! She was aghast at the thought that she was ever going to be this old and wrinkled. On the other hand, she had all her limbs and seemed to be quite healthy for her age.

"Lordy, Lordy, I'd forgotten!" the old woman cackled, clearly delighted at the sight of Fifi.

"I beg your pardon?" Boston Fifi inquired politely.

"No time!" the old woman retorted. "Quick, you had a question. What was it?"

"What is my purpose in life?" Fifi asked. Thank heavens she'd remembered.

"Oh yes," the old woman sighed, relieved. "Wholly masseuse."

"Wholly what?"

"Well, fairly wholly," the old woman amended as the room began to fade.

"What?!" Fifi pleaded.

"Wholly masseuse!" a tiny voice piped as Fifi found herself being pulled back by the silver cord, back down to the lake and then up over the mountains.

Wholly masseuse? What did that mean? And Fifi *hated* massage.

Fifi was back in the cave with Bo-ku. His eyes were open, and he was smiling at her. He reached out and touched her third eye with his right middle finger. Fifi felt all of her, inside and out, begin to glisten.

"Congratulations, you have your answer," Bo complimented her.

"But it was wrong–I mean, I'm afraid I didn't understand it," Fifi protested.

Bo said nothing. He gently took her hand, began chanting, and a moment later they were back in the city beside the little stream, awaiting her first customer.

Oh no, it was Apu, the same old man as before! Whatever you feared, you drew toward you, Bo kept telling her, but this was ridiculous. At first Fifi just wanted to bolt again. The smell. Those ugly sores. Apu's near nakedness.

But then…Bo was lightly kneading Apu's body and gently cupping his hands over Apu's chakras. Apu, eyes closed, breathed deeply, sighed and began to smile. What Bo was doing was beautiful, healing. Something was happening between Bo and Apu that was so–so *exquisite*.

Massage to Bo-ku was a fierce and delicate art which encompassed the whole of the human experience–from the most delicious delights of the physical to the headiest heights of the spiritual. The real healing came from the energy flowing through the body more than the physical rubbing.

Bo-ku gave Fifi two simple tasks when they worked together. Her first job was to breathe deeply and allow Pure White Light to flow in through the crown of her head, down her arms, out through her hands and into her patient. Her second job was to "listen" with her fingers–to allow to emerge all the emotions and feelings, all the dark and all the light things, that were waiting eagerly under her patient's skin. From under all of them she could draw forth Healing. If she just opened herself to the Light and "listened" to her partner, she'd know what to do.

And gradually, over time, her talent did begin to emerge. Bo-ku would lay his hands gently on her as she waved her hands over her patient. Fifi soon began to be able to feel the chakras. As long as she had Bo to guide her, when she placed her hands over two of the magic points on her patient's body and closed her eyes, she'd feel as though ten thousand years of wisdom were flowing through her fingers. Then she'd play, she'd swoop, she'd dance with her patient's innermost being, until their fourteen energy centers were swirling merrily around the Universe, lit with a pleasant glow.

During one of these sessions she realized that she was born to be a masseuse who massaged souls, rather than bodies—a holy masseuse. And suddenly the phrase her future self had told her—"wholly masseuse"—made perfect sense.

She spent a happy year and a half with Bo-ku. They were blessed with two lovely daughters, baby Edna, born, oddly enough, with purple hair, and baby Ethel, with pink locks. Since Fifi had, basically, no parenting skills—and no desire to do to her children what had been done to her—at Bo-ku's suggestion she allowed the girls to be adopted. They chose the lucky parents by following their inner sight. Edna was adopted by a most interesting couple visiting from Moonee Ponds, Australia; and Ethel was handed off to a safely non-descript pair from Lesser Tuna, Texas. Three months later, his work done, Bo-ku died.

There's no need to break it to you gently. While lounging comfortably in Fifi's loving arms, Bo-ku deliberately and consciously "departed the physical" on his seventy-fourth birthday, in an inspiring ceremony, sold out months in advance, before two hundred thousand of his closest devotees. Fifi felt an intense surge of energy as dear Bo's soul slipped out of his body.

Fifi rejected the popular misconception that she'd enjoy joining Bo-ku on his funeral pyre. "Thanks, but no thanks," was Fifi's feeling. She used the remainder of Bo's departing energy to clear a broad path through the crowd. Those who have seen Charlton Heston, playing Moses parting the Red Sea, will have some idea of the scene. Fifi zipped down the path and escaped down the Ganges with a tittering troupe of temple transvestites.

Like so many young widows, she faced a tough career choice. Should she go back to Boston and settle into the life of an unpopular but pampered idle aristocrat, or should she spend arduous years perfecting her massage skills? Fifi made her choice. She remained in India, attaching herself to the court of a convenient Rajah. She was prepared to tackle chakras. She found herself confronting sex.

Fifi Faces Down Sex

One evening shortly after she joined the court, Fifi found herself with Rahul, a member of the Rajah's personal guard. Rahul was a handsome, strapping gentleman seeking relief from lower back pain. Fifi did a moderately competent job of balancing his chakras from the back and then had him turn over. Fifi couldn't help noticing that he was exceedingly attractive. She wondered if now might be a good time to work on overcoming her one chakra-massage shortcoming.

Bo-ku had always emphasized that the Road to Healing and the Path to Paradise wound through the body's seven chakras, the first of which, as careful inspection shows, is located right in the heart of the groin, midway between the genitals and the anus. Fifi had always skipped this one. All Fifi had to do to start, Bo had kept insisting, was simply cup her right palm over her client's first chakra and keep it there until she was calm. She needn't do anything else.

It had sounded easy enough. The few times Fifi had tried it, however, the intense surges of very mixed feelings had been too much for her. Her face had gotten red; sweat had broken out on her forehead; her mouth had gone dry; her hand had started to tremble; and she'd quickly snatched it away. Even with Bo's help, she hadn't been able to handle it. She'd worked with chakras two through seven, but not the first. That part of the body was evil! And what would her patients think?!

A lesser instructor would have insisted Fifi do it the "right" way. Bo-ku told her to take her time, go only as fast as seemed enjoyable.

But now Bo was gone. Fifi looked down at the comely Rahul. By golly, if she was going to be a holy masseuse, she was going to have to learn to handle all the chakras sometime. The fact that Rahul was young and attractive added the necessary incentive.

Rahul, turning over onto his back, found Fifi's nervous right hand cupped gingerly between his legs. He then felt her left hand waving rather shakily over the center of his chest, above his heart chakra.

Rahul had never felt electric tingling sensations such as this. He sprang eagerly to attention. Even through his clothes it was quite evident. Fifi almost let her right hand stray boldly onto his member; instead she just kept it cupped over his first chakra, closed her eyes, breathed deeply and visualized healing. Next thing she knew, she and Rahul were both achieving amazing orgasms. When Rahul returned to Earthly awareness, he found his back was better than new, and he was being goggled at by a very smitten Fifi. Hastily muttering, "Thank you. Very good. Very good," Rahul forked over a donation of rupees and made his escape.

Fifi flopped onto her pallet. She was aghast at what she'd done; yet visions of sugarplums danced naked through her imagination. Men for millennia have accused women of "falling in love too fast." Fifi, at least, was guilty as charged.

When would she see this absolute heartthrob again? Would it be too bold of her to offer him an immediate "freebie?" Should she invite him to dinner? (It was a tad too soon, she felt, to begin hinting at marriage). The next afternoon Fifi "accidentally" found herself strolling past the guard room when Rahul emerged with a couple of his fellow guards. Doing an excellent imitation of a man spying a she-demon, Rahul quickly averted his eyes and rushed his cronies off down a side corridor without a single word of tender greeting. Fifi rushed back to her trusty pallet and threw herself on it, grief-stricken.

"He thinks I'm a...a whore!" Fifi sobbed. "I *am* a whore, a big ugly whore!" All the things her parents and Boston society had drummed into her came thumping through her head. Fifi spent a horrible night, feeling lonely and ugly and evil and rejected.

But in the morning Fifi rallied. Her grief had worked itself out. She knew she was a good and worthwhile person, even if what had happened with Rahul wasn't right, and even if their romance wasn't to be. She was going to face this first chakra thing and lick it. She'd just be more careful in the future, that's all.

For her next first-chakra experiment, figuring she'd be safer with a member of her own sex, Fifi cupped her right hand over the groin of an attractive young lady who made her living as a temple dancer. Again, double intense explosions. Again the patient was cured. Again Fifi was rebuffed when she proposed Romance (but it didn't hurt as much this time).

Unfortunately, the Rajah's Principal Wife had overheard the ecstatic cries issuing from Fifi's workchamber. The ensuing scandal absolutely mortified Fifi. She was a healer who'd "taken advantage of" her patients. She scurried to Bangkok, where for almost six months she avoided the first chakra. Then, again, scandal led Fifi to flee, this time to Africa.

For the next half-century or so, Fifi zigzagged around the world perfecting her skills. She practiced her trade wherever she felt herself drawn, fleeing whenever involuntary orgasms caused another ruckus (especially when they happened on a deathbed with friends and family gathered round). Except for her continued fear of sex, gradually all her old prejudices disappeared.

Wealth, race, station in life meant nothing any longer to our holy masseuse. She found the wrong side of Cape Town or Cairo as intriguing as the Right Bank of Paris. Old or young, rich or poor, ugly or beautiful, it didn't matter to Fifi. In the realms where she operated, the externals were irrelevant. She was nearly as happy in Buckingham Palace as she was in her favorite AIDS hospice.

Then, a year ago, her long-forgotten daughter Ethel, having hired detectives to track her down, flew to Egypt and invited Fifi to come visit her at her palatial Bev Hills estate. She'd only been there two days when Ethel brought in a slightly befuddled middle-aged geek and announced, "Mom, meet Edna's son. He's your grandson Strange! Strange, say hi to your Granny Fifi!"

I Meet My Doom

As Aunt Ethel said, "Strange, say hi to your Granny Fifi," we both stood back, sizing each other up. I had no idea I was meeting the woman with whom I would, within the year, be arrested for murder and prostitution. I'd never heard of Filonia Fulbright Bo-ku, knew none of the history you've just read. I'm trying to think back to exactly how it was. I know the whole thing only took a few seconds.

"Ethel nabbed you too, huh?" Granny Fifi chuckled. "Two days ago I was healing people in the slums of Cairo. Then she swooped me up, and here I am."

"You heal people?"

"For sixty-odd years," Granny Fi proclaimed proudly. She demonstrated in the air in front of her how she directed energy through patients' bodies, and I told her I was a masseur in San Francisco and found directing energy to be the most magical part.

"Maybe it runs in families," Granny Fifi mused. That's when it happened.

"OHO!" Aunt Ethel exclaimed. "My nips are tingling! Wait. Wait. I know what it is...You two should work on someone together! And I know just exactly who the lucky #1 should be."

"What!?" I'd been looking forward to lying around the pool with movie stars, not working with my new Granny Shrek.

Fifi looked me up and down, and agreed that she was much too tired.

"Well, maybe just to break the ice, you could each do a private session with him first, and then later work on him together," Ethel cooed.

"Oh, Ethel, pumpkin, I'd love to," Fifi interrupted, "but I'm afraid I'm not quite up to it this morning."

"What a pity," the Baroness countered. "And Jason's irresistible too."

"Oh, really?" Fifi replied politely. Then, when the wily Baroness (super salesperson that she was) remained maddeningly silent, she was forced to add, "How so?"

The Baroness paused to consider."Maybe it's his curly blond hair. Fresh-smelling blond. Sort of surfer blond, I suppose you might say. And then those big melting ice-blue eyes. I swear, you just want to jump right in and drown."

My ears pricked up, but I continued looking out in the direction of the pool, too timid to interrupt.

"What else?" Ethel mused. "Oh yes, tanned silky skin, one of those cleverly V-shaped torsos, and an endowment–not that you're interested, of course–an endowment that makes Harvard's look like pretty small potatoes. And so vigorous! Well, most young men of eighteen are."

"Eighteen!" Fifi exclaimed, visibly wavering.

"He's a student, of course–at one of those wholesome Midwestern universities. And..." The Baroness paused significantly.

"Yes?" Fifi urged in spite of herself. I was gritting my teeth, pretending not to listen. Ethel knew so much about my life; was she teasing me, too, on purpose?

"Oh, I just thought I'd mention that he'll be on the U.S. gymnastics team at the Olympics this summer. Yes," the Baroness resumed, driving the thing home. "If I had to sum Jason up in ten words or less, I suppose I'd say he's a simply scrumptious Olympic gymnast with an enormously amusing sexual problem."

An amusing sexual problem too?! Oh my! No one enjoyed a good laugh more than Fifi. Up to this point she'd been determined to resist. After all, in her work it didn't matter what her patients looked like. She needn't be swayed by mere youth and physical beauty. However, Jason did sound enticing. And since Ethel's nipples had actually tingled...

"Now you do have me intrigued," Fifi admitted. "And, of course, if it would help the Olympic effort..."

"I'll send a jet and have him here this afternoon."

Jason Tolliver McVeer
Step Right Up to the Blond Angel

18 Years Ago. "Oh!" Fat Fanny gushed. "Would you look at that curly blond hair and those big blue eyes! You're just a little Angel. I sure do want to take you home with me. Oh, yes I do! Oh, yes I do!"

The baby in question, little Jason Tolliver McVeer, stared up at her with his enormous, trusting, fun-filled baby blues. You looked into those orbs; you were a goner. Jason had most assuredly emerged from the womb a charmer, with all the world his snake.

After a spell, Fat Fanny reluctantly handed the boychild back to his mother, Ruby "Rings" McVeer. Ruby was the premiere trapeze artist with the Cucumber Family Circus. Both Ruby and the Circus had recently settled down: she with tightrope walker Wayne "Stroller" McVeer; the psychedelic circus family to a farming commune in Croutch, Arkansas. Enough traveling around the country! Let the customers come to them.

The Cukes were enamored with Robert Heinlein's *Stranger in a Strange Land*, the book often credited with having started the "New Age" movement. The troupe based their communal living arrangement on Heinlein's "Nest," where everyone lived naked, loved each other in twos and threes, and occasionally had entire group sharings. Among the Cukes, anyone might sleep with anyone; and, every Saturday night, everyone did.

There were problems, of course. The Cukes were no strangers to jealousy, hurt feelings, anguish, even fights. And adjustments had to be made, naturally, for individual quirks. The Snake Man's scales, for example. And Fat Fanny's flatulence, let's face it, was a trial to everyone.

Still, casual, comfy group sex was an accepted Cuke lifestyle. In Croutch, if you dropped in on Jason's parents, Wayne and Ruby, you might find a number of naked folks, lounging around, chatting and laughing and stroking each other. Is it any wonder Jason ended up believing that bodies were perfectly natural?

As Jason grew, he became one of those dynamos who tear around all out and then suddenly curl up and go to sleep...and then tear around some more. From babyhood he loved stimulation of any kind. He loved the feel of sunlight on his bare skin. He loved to roll in the grass or throw himself headlong into the river. Whatever the sensation, Jason wanted to feel it over as much of himself as he could. You couldn't keep clothes on him.

Au naturel, which is how he usually was, you'd notice at once that he had *quite* the penis, which, as soon as he could talk, he insisted on naming Buster. Buster proved a problem even for the free-thinking, free-loving Cukes.

Adults having sex with each other was fine, but with a child?! They would have avoided the issue if they could, but Buster was like a friendly Irish setter puppy who loved to be petted. When Jason was being rubbed, he wasn't thinking. He was giving himself up totally to the sensation. So he'd just present you with Buster unconsciously–while, like as not, looking trustfully up at you with those great big periwinkle blues. How could you destroy his Innocence by telling him there was something wrong with his body? It went against everything the Cukes believed. They talked it over in a group meeting and decided they would raise Jason without shame. They would touch Buster. Jason could touch them, but not to orgasm. Actual sex would be just one of those things reserved for grownups.

Meanwhile, Jason became a bona fide circus performer. He could be seen, in a striking spangled outfit, cavorting on Daddy's shoulders as Wayne strolled lightly across the high wire. Jason loved the attention. "Look at me! Look at me! Look at me!" his entire being shouted. From Wayne and Ruby, Jason had inherited perfect balance, and, not just a lack of fear, but a perfect *love* of heights.

When Jason grew old enough to start public school, however, he had to be taught conventional prohibitions. Whether Jason was doing anything immoral or not, he was leading his adult friends into something very illegal–with a capital Hard Labor. Jason's (or even his parents') consent made no difference. If it could be proven that someone had petted Buster, that someone would be breaking rocks on a chain gang for twenty to thirty-five years. That would be horrible.

Jason resolved that it was *his* responsibility to prevent such a disaster from happening. As soon as he was aware that Buster might be touched, he'd call a halt. Ruby, Wayne and the Cukes all heaved a big sigh of regret and relief.

Jason's new policy was easy in theory but nearly impossible in practice. Well, put yourself in Jason's place. It felt so good to be touched. He liked to abandon himself, mindlessly, to the pleasure. And how was he going to explain things to poor, innocent, friendly Buster?

Yet, there was no way around it. As soon as he was aware of what he was doing, he had to quit.

So it became a race against himself. Buster tried to cram in as much pleasure as he could before Jason's conscience kicked in and made him stop. It worked fairly well until Jason and Buster hit puberty.

Puberty Is Hit, Out of the Ballpark

Jason must have stood on a stool, because he reached man's estate a full year before the other boys his age. And Buster did too, with all the reticence of a big, friendly, adolescent Irish setter, eagerly humping your leg.

"Here comes Jason," someone would cry.

"And Buster," someone else would be sure to add. They were quite a team.

"That boy's a pop-tart," the "looser" element of Croutch chuckled. The "decent" element took a dimmer view. Ruby McVeer found herself visited by Croutch's first female Revised Southern Baptist minister, the righteous Reverend Molly Mae Gibbs.

"Ruby, you've got to do something about that boy of yours," the agitated Reverend opened. She hadn't knocked. Not even a "How do you do?" She'd just barged right in. Ruby was a little annoyed, but it did give her an excuse to postpone the ironing.

"What do you mean, Molly Mae?"

"It ain't decent for a boy to run around like that."

"Like what?" Ruby asked (though she knew full well like what; she just wanted to make Molly Mae say it).

Molly Mae took the bull by the horns. "Sticking out like that. It ain't decent."

"But what can he do, Molly Mae? He doesn't *mean* to do it."

Just then Jason banged in through the back door, and Ruby told him why Mrs. Gibbs had called. Jason walked right up to Molly Mae and looked at her as honestly as she'd ever been looked at in her life. "I can't help it, Ma'am," Jason said. "And I don't think it's wrong." His big blue eyes said he spoke nothing but what was so, and his halo glowed. Molly Mae had the transfixed look of a religious rabbit caught in God's Headlights. She found herself receiving Truth from an Angel.

Molly Mae left, a changed woman. Jason was right. Ruby was right. How could you discipline a lad for not suppressing a God-given function? You couldn't. In fact, Molly Mae didn't recover her senses until Sunday morning–halfway through a sermon declaring the human body to be the beautiful Temple of the Lord. Our Molly hastily called for the closing hymn and then fled to her study to try to figure out what in the world had happened to her.

As for Jason, he was saddened to think Miz Gibbs was scared of Buster. He was always a little embarrassed when Buster decided to sit up and beg in public. It caused strangers to act funny at first. But it happened all the time, and there was nothing he could do to hide it. He learned to live with it.

And so did Croutch. Most people, in fact, rather grew to enjoy it. Among his classmates–indeed, among the population at large–all the girls and, well, all the boys had crushes on Jason.

For a brief time in his early teens, as the juices started to flow and most people were beginning to appear very much more attractive to him, Jason had begun to find some other people very much *less* attractive. Even ugly. Some people had actually repulsed him. Looking at them sexually had made a difference.

He'd faced the problem squarely. He just plain didn't think it was right to find anyone repulsive, so he'd offered himself to the "ugly" ones. In his mind Jason believed no one could be repulsive, so he'd practiced with his body until he believed it in his mind and heart as well.

Jason had one precious healing gift to give. That gift was himself, and he gave it freely and naturally to anyone who could accept it. You could love Jason freely and honorably. Jason believed so firmly it was all right to trust you, that darned if you didn't believe it yourself. You wouldn't dream of violating Jason or his trust. It was an amazing talent, and most of Croutch loved him for it.

"He's just an Angel!" the vast majority declared.

"And he *looks* so innocent!" the minuscule minority complained.

Meanwhile, Jason was developing into an impressive athlete. Baseball, football, wrestling, track–Jason loved using his body. And he loved being watched by a crowd. He seemed to soak up all that concentrated attention right through his skin.

It was at gymnastics that he really shone. After all, Jason had been playing with acrobats ever since he was born. Jason was state all-around champion three years running.

He was also a knockout. By the time Jason was ready for college, you could have stood him up against a bust of the young Alexander the Great, and (except for having a nose) Jason could easily have passed for Young Alex's handsomer, healthier, younger brother–one who was a very much more peaceable sort and worked out just a little harder at the gym.

Jason had his choice of colleges. He decided to accept a scholarship from the large midwestern university that had, in his opinion, the country's best gymnastics team.

But would the university be able to deal with an outstanding student who stood out most noticeably around the middle? And, though we've discussed a little of Jason's sexual nature, we haven't yet mentioned his sexual problem, the one the Baroness Ethelina had found so amusing and distressing.

An Amusing Sexual Problem

"Psst, here comes Jason!" Mindy Morke hissed to her two Tri-Delt sisters as they stood gossiping on the steps of the sorority.

Naomi Dolan automatically stood straighter, took a deep breath and pulled back her shoulders. Helen "Hooter" Troy, a newcomer to the campus, said, "Who's Ja...Whoa!"

Hooter's mouth dropped open. There was a God, and He'd just granted her dearest wish. "Oh my!" she breathed.

The cause of this excitement loped up cheerfully. Jason was feeling the warm spring sunshine on his bare chest and being buoyed up by the sight and smell of the fresh green grass. "Hey, Mindy, how ya doin'? Hi, Naomi." He looped his arms around the two and gave them quick kisses. They'd each asked him to be their boyfriend, but, having been raised with honor, Jason refused to make promises he couldn't keep. He'd made it clear to the whole campus that he wasn't ready to settle down. Jason believed in loving everybody. And, having greeted the two he'd already enjoyed, he now looked expectantly at the third of the three Tri-Delts.

"Oh!" Mindy exclaimed, surfacing from a refreshing dip into Jason's baby blues to find herself caught between her clear social duty and the realization that Hooter Troy was the very *last* rival to whom she wanted to introduce her Romeo.

"This is Hooter Troy," she announced resignedly.

"Hi, Hooter," Jason acknowledged. Hooter? Jason was widely known as a "tit man." And there was no need to ask where Hooter had acquired her nickname.

"We're going to watch you on tv tomorrow," Mindy gushed. The whole campus was keyed-up over the big meet.

"I called home to California," Naomi threw in, "to tell my folks to watch. National television now and the Olympics next summer. Wow!" What she wouldn't give to drag Jason off to someplace secluded right about now.

Jason grinned at his well-wishers and then moved a strategic two steps closer to Hooter. "How do you like it so far?" he asked amiably.

Hooter was caught off guard. Oh, how did she like the *campus*, he meant. "I like it just fine," she replied, allowing her chest to sway just a little. She let her eyes pout their lips and whisper huskily, "Hello, Sailor."

"Hey, maybe I can give you a little tour," Jason offered brightly, always wanting to do the helpful thing.

"Why, that'd be great," Hooter agreed, wiggling her chest just the teensiest little bit more and turning her gaze up to search and destroy. My goodness, a surge of activity in Jason's cut-offs made it more than plain that he'd noticed.

"How about meeting me after gymnastics practice," Jason suggested. "Say four o'clock in front of the gym?"

"I'll be there," Hooter promised breathily.

"Oh, girls!" Hooter sighed as her new suitor galloped off. "And did you notice...?"

"It happens to him all the time," Mindy snapped testily.

After Hooter scooted off to French class, Naomi muttered, "*C'est la vie*. He had to meet her sometime. Do you think we should have warned her, though?"

"No!" Mindy replied, with just a trace of ladylike malice. "Let her find out for herself." They tramped righteously off to Modern Ethics.

Jason, meanwhile, was just entering the locker room. "Hi, guys," he called.

"Hey, Jason! Hey, Killer! Hey, dude!" were a few of the verbal responses, and Jason also received his usual quota of friendly claps and slaps on shoulders, back and, especially, ass. Jason's influence had expanded the team members' sexual horizons beyond all recognition.

But this afternoon, Jason was preoccupied. Practice went by in a blur. Promptly at four, he met Hooter in front of the gym. By four twelve they were in his apartment, and he was showing her the campus's primary item of interest. You can guess what it was.

"Oh, Hooter," Jason moaned, fumbling under her sweater. "Mmm slurble mumph."

"Oh, baby doll," Hooter giggled happily, running her fingers through Jason's angel locks. It was awesome. There actually seemed to be *light* around Jason's head.

Then Jason kissed her. And when Jason kissed you, he wasn't doing *anything* else. Hooter had heard of knees turning to rubber. This was the first time she'd gotten to enjoy the sensation first hand.

And then she found herself naked, and Jason was sniffing and touching and tasting and feeling her whole body! No young man had ever been so taken with Hooter–so enthusiastic, so absolutely bowled over by her physical charms. Jason was lost in her body–licking and laughing and going, "Mmm, mmm, mmph."

Have you ever been so horny you positively couldn't stand it–couldn't talk, couldn't think, could hardly breathe? Have you ever been so caught up in passion, so turned on, you just had to achieve union right now? That's the way Jason felt; because that's the way he always felt when he was in bed with anyone. He dove into the sight, the taste, the feel, the smell of Hooter. His own body writhed and rubbed and twined around his partner's. Oh my God! This time...!

"Aargh, oops, sorry," Jason groaned.

"Wha'?" Hooter asked. She looked down and discovered Jason's little "problem."

It was a pity. Jason had the body, the reflexes and the training of a world-class gymnast. He should have been a superb lover. He even knew, he could feel, all the moves he wanted to make. He'd race like mad to get at least some of them in before Buster went off half-cocked, but Buster would breast the tape before him every time.

It was so frustrating! He longed for sex, ached for sex, could think of nothing *but* sex. He just couldn't *have* sex. He was like a man perpetually dying of thirst, who, time after agonizing time, clutches the glass of life-giving water so tightly it shatters before he can bring it to his lips.

"What's wrong, Jason?" his roommate Jock asked when he got in from his date.

"Oh, Jock, I met a girl named Hooter today, and she was so nice, and..."

"The usual?"

"Yeah."

"That's tough," Jock sympathized. He plopped down on the couch beside his roommate and threw a comforting arm around his shoulder. Jason smelled Jock and the lingering traces of Jock's date.

"Oops, sorry," Jason grunted a few moments later.

"That's ok, dude," Jock replied. He handed Jason a towel.

"I wish I knew where to go for help," Jason sighed.

As it turned out he didn't have to go anywhere. Help was already on its way.

A Baroness Is Inspired

The Baroness Ethelina was lying in bed skimming the latest issue of *Vanity Fair*, while Fred was watching some sort of sports show on the wall-sized tv. Ethel was just jotting down the name of a refreshingly unspoiled-looking young actor it would be refreshing to track down and spoil, when she heard the tv announcer say something about a "young Arkansas Adonis."

The next moment her nipples were being jolted by 20,000 volts of Pure Inspiration, and her lips were screeching, "FRED, WHO'S THAT?! He's...he's my Mystery Romeo!"

The following afternoon found Ethel's private jet landing at the airport serving the large midwestern university where Jason Tolliver McVeer topped, as it were, the gymnastics team's award-winning totem pole. As her rented limo toted her smoothly campus-ward, Ethel giggled to herself. She loved playing the good fairy, and she could just see the look of delight on Jason's face when he learned he was about to go–there was no other way of putting it–from unknown college student to the Hottest Movie Star in the World.

"This is it," the rented chauffeur announced, pulling up in front of a run-down, two-bedroom, faded-yellow house. Ethel checked herself carefully in the mirror before allowing herself to be helped from the back seat. She'd gone incognito in a four-thousand-dollar sweatsuit and a mere quarter mil in jewels.

Telling her bodyguard to stay in the car, she trotted eagerly up the walk and pressed the bell. Jason answered the door wearing only a ragged pair of gym shorts.

"Oh my!" Ethel remarked appreciatively. His minimalist clothing statement struck her as inspired.

Jason grinned and eyed Ethel, also appreciatively. He seemed to be paying special attention to the brooches pinned over her ample right breast (bunch your attractions, was Ethel's motto).

"I'm Ethel von Elm," the Baroness announced, thrusting out her bejeweled right hand. To herself she thought, "Those eyes! Easy now, Ethel." To Jason she said, "Just call me Ethel."

"Come in," Jason invited.

"Woof! Look at those boobies!" barked Buster.

"Can I get you a carrot juice?" Jason asked. "Coffee? Beer?" Damn, were there any of those cookies left? He hadn't expected to be entertaining a world-famous Baroness.

"A beer would be nice," Ethel said. It was such fun going incognito.

When they were settled in on the somewhat ragged couch, Jason asked seductively yet sincerely, "What can I do for you?" He sat holding her hand as though she were just anybody and gazing into her eyes as though she were just Everybody.

Ethel had planned to lead up to it, but as she melted under that gaze, she blurted it right out. "You're the Mystery Romeo in my new movie!"

Jason's heart jumped. My God! This was unbelievable. Everyone was always telling him he could be a movie star, and he'd wanted to give it a shot after the Olympics. And now he was going to start out as the star of the biggest movie ever! "Jesus!" he enthused. "That's amazing! Thank you, Mrs. von Elm!"

Before she could remind him again to call her Ethel, he threw his arms around his benefactress and squished her to him joyfully. Ethel couldn't help feeling something large against her ample middle. Was it his knee or his penis? She looked down. Good Lord! It wasn't his knee.

"Buster's excited too," Jason explained.

Was Buster who she thought he was? And should she…Oh no, she couldn't. Ethel was no stranger to extramarital flings, but Jason was far too young.

"How did you pick me?" Jason demanded.

"Well, Honey, I saw you on tv, and my nipples tingled."

"Oh, wow!" Jason breathed. Everyone knew about Ethel's psychic nipples.

"Mmm," he added, "you smell good."

"Do I?" Ethel found that fact marvelous. Bless Liz Taylor for going into the perfume business.

"Mmm," Jason said.

What happened next wasn't because she was rich, Ethel was sure, or because she'd just handed Jason the world on a platter with watercress around it. It was because he *liked* her. It was because he liked *her*. She'd slept with a lot of men, but no one had ever desired her the way Jason did. It was a miracle that *she* was the woman he was in love with.

Well, somehow she found that her movie plans had faded from her consciousness, and her sweatsuit and Jason's tattered shorts had slipped to the floor, and she was about to be filled by the biggest…

And then she heard, "GRAUGGHH! Oops! Oh, shit!"

"What's wrong?" Ethel gasped dazedly. Even though Jason hadn't actually entered her, she'd felt a huge jolt of energy through her vagina and nipples for about a microsecond.

"Oh, this always happens," Jason moaned.

And when she realized what had happened, Ethel started laughing. "I'm sorry, honeybun," she apologized. "It just struck me funny. You should have seen your face!" And off she went into another round of guffaws, which were so infectious Jason found himself joining in.

"I guess it is sort of funny," Jason admitted. If he couldn't cure his troubles, at least he'd found someone who could help him laugh at them.

After they'd dressed, Ethel got down to business. It would be almost a year before they started shooting the film, and Jason must agree to keep the whole affair secret. Naturally, Jason and Ethel celebrated their arrangement with champagne fetched from the waiting limo. Again, the fizz on the bubbly lasted considerably longer than Jason. (Though he did, to please her, manage to call Mrs. von Elm "Ethel" twice, before he inadvertently came.)

As they were lying in bed afterwards, an innocent comment of Jason's revealed that he wasn't actually in love with Ethel. He desired everyone that way. At first Ethel was crushed, but later, in the limo, she grasped the staggering artistic and commercial possibilities of an Angel Who Loves Everyone.

"The public will go ga-ga!" Ethel exulted as she jetted home. "He *is* an Angel. Up there on the screen he'll be, he'll be…absolutely *Inspiring*!

Little did Ethel imagine that the very next evening, her wayward husband Fred was about to be inspired by a performer of a very different kind.

Zelda Mishimoto
An Amazonian Goddess Makes Her Kyoto Debut

Seventeen men of ten nationalities were seated in the posh private theater of a serene and impressive mansion outside Kyoto. Several owned smallish countries. One owned a medium-sized country. Five were royal in the worldly sense. One was a Prince of the Church. "Captains of finance and industry" summed up most of the rest. And then there was Baron Frederick von Elm.

The assembled had come for the dancing debut of an already infamous young student of the classical School for Mininuko Courtesans. Her name was Zelda Mishimoto.

Fred had first heard of Zelda from a drunken acquaintance in a hotel lobby in Tangier. While Fred had tried to shush him, his informant had blubbered on and on about this amazing young temptress and the mind-boggling erotic tricks she was willing, nay avid, to perform. Since the man in question was a short, older, tubby fellow, such as himself, Fred realized this Zelda would likely be willing to do the same sorts of things with him. And Ethel, well, Ethel had been distracted with her own projects for far too long. Fred had never strayed before, but he felt he deserved a new playmate, too.

Ethel, lulled into a false sense of security by an untroubled forty-year reign, didn't even notice the perspiration on her turtle dove's brow and his tell-tale stammer as he nervously mentioned he thought he might, uh, attend, um, an interesting, er, computer conference in Japan. And now, here he was in Kyoto!

Upon entering the Mishimoto Mansion, Fred had felt a momentary visceral lurch as the pair of diffident servants (actually two of Papa-san's deadly ninja bodyguards), while bowing respectfully, had automatically plotted out thirty-seven efficient methods of ending his life. "Must be something I ate," Fred had decided.

All the guests were led off to be bathed, massaged and mildly titillated by Mininuko Courtesans, either full-fledged or apprentice. Only one of said seventeen guests was inadvertently allowed to reach climax. All were now softened up (or perhaps that's not quite the term) for the evening's entertainment.

The lights dimmed; an eminent *shakuhachi* artist began producing eerily beautiful music that drifted softly into the listeners' very beings. Gradually dancers and dragons and God-knows-what-all began shimmering in from nowhere, floating around intriguingly for a bit and then disappearing. If Ethel had dragged Fred to one night of experimental theater, she'd dragged him to a thousand, but tonight's lighting and special effects were like nothing he'd ever seen. All the audience members were entranced.

I know none of this is really happening, the guests kept assuring themselves, but still they found themselves edging over into that magical state of mind where fairy tales do come true.

And then *She* appeared. Some of the powerhouses in the audience actually began to wonder if they weren't presumptuous just to aspire. Fred certainly did.

Yet Zelda, perhaps to allay those fears, began by grounding her dance in the earth itself, with the simple beauties of nature. She was the swan swimming, the wild goose flying, the leaf borne gracefully upon the wind. Only then did she enter the human realm. She was a baby, a child, a young virgin, a young virgin awakening.

Other dancers joined Zelda. And then it got a touch confusing. Were those two naked gentlemen trying to save Zelda from being ravished by the large golden dragon, for instance, or vice versa?

At last the other characters disappeared, and Zelda, alone and naked, gave herself up to the Dance. She was woman. She was man. She was goddess. She was demon. She was fire. She was ice. Exotic, otherworldly, mysterious, Zelda absolutely commanded the stage.

Out of the Dance, Zelda looked into the eyes of each member of the audience. How long did she look? A too-brief eternity, most would have replied. She looked as long as necessary, until she felt that internal click, that lift, that surge of ultra-erotic, yet more than merely erotic, ecstasy. She looked as long as it took her pale-violet eyes to make, honestly, the Mininuko Promise: "Yes, I could truly love you. Yes, I do truly love you. Love is All."

Each jaded man in turn found his heart bursting into flame, his insides turning to butter. Each man in turn found himself a new and better man. Fred flamed and melted with the best.

When the dance was finished, the princes and captains flocked, like swallows hell-bent for Capistrano, to Papa-san at the back of the salon to sign up for an evening of Zelda's private services at however many million yen it took. Papa-san gleefully began filling Zelda's appointment book.

Fred, meanwhile, was at a loss. He'd have paid anything to make Zelda his this very night, but by the time he could squirm through the seething throng, she was already booked. He had to make do with the first available date, six weeks away in Paris, where Zelda was scheduled to dance at a "do" being given by one of the Rothschilds.

"I'll take it!" he squeaked. And then he flew back home to Ethel.

It's Raining Goddesses

17 years ago, in the upper Upper Amazon. Chief Jahgla arrived, panting.

"What thing happen?!" he demanded.

"Great silver bird fall from sky, BOOM-BOOM." Gigla reported. "Drop girlchild next me."

The Chief looked at Gigla, who since the death of the last medicine man some weeks ago had been rather hastily promoted.

The Chief took in the creamy skin and violet eyes of the squalling girlchild. He was a man who knew how to get right to the heart of a matter. "Goddess?" he demanded. "Or," he added, surreptitiously making the sign to ward off evil, "she be Demon?"

"I no know," Gigla started to say.

However, his teacher Banquo, the old witch doctor, had impressed upon him that he must always appear to know what he was doing. "Bluff your way through," had been Banquo's general-purpose advice. Remembering the brief glimpse of perfect trust in the girlchild's eyes, Gigla decided to take a chance. "Skin sacred color of clouds. Eyes color of orchids. Goddess," Gigla announced.

The Chief bought it. "Girlchild! Goddess!" he proudly informed the rest of the tribe, as they came pounding up. "I raise like own daughter."

And so the baby was carried back to the village and handed over to a tribeslady who was already nursing her own baby. This good lady, never having read Dr. Spock's excellent manual on the care and feeding of young cloud-skinned Goddesses, was overawed. A Goddess! Within a couple of days she'd nicknamed the bright active child Zel-da, "Little Monkey," and was raising her as one of her own.

As she grew, Zel-da became a sprightly elflike little gamin, always darting about and asking questions, forever poking into everything. She was also acutely sensitive to emotions. She was empathic, not telepathic. Zel-da couldn't read minds, but she could see auras. By the color and changing patterns of the lights around your body, she could tell how you were feeling. When you were happy, she gleefully shared your joy. When you were sad, even though you tried to hide it, she knew, and she'd cuddle up and comfort you.

But it was Gigla who continued to fascinate her. She was drawn to his knowledge (limited though it was) of the supernatural, of the spirit world. She loved to pitter-patter after him out into the jungle and help him gather roots and herbs and whatnot. She loved to notice how funny things were and titter about it with him. She loved to sit in his hut and watch him prepare his charms and medicines.

How old would she be, the Chief wanted to know, before she started making Goddess Magic–taming wild beasts, calling down lightning from the sky, casually looking at people and causing them to burst into flames?

Gigla couldn't answer him. But one morning when she was five, Zel-da got into Gigla's secret stash of psychedelic *epena*, and the Goddess reawakened.

All Hell Breaks Loose

It seemed like an ordinary morning, which just goes to show you. Gigla and the other men were out hunting; the women were busy fixing brunch; so the children decided to play Grownup.

The tribe had never experienced venereal disease. Nor had they made the tricky connection between intercourse and pregnancy. So for them sex was simply fun-fun. Like our closest relatives in the animal kingdom, the bonobo, all the adults engaged in foreplay or sex several times a day, and their partner might be any other adult of either gender. In Zel-da's new tribe, everybody was naked and cuddled with everyone else.

When a warrior was in the mood, for instance, he'd just stroll, love club displayed at the ready, down Main Street, hoping to attract some willing attention.

So this particular morning three boys sauntered down Main Street acting the part of warriors in heat (except that they had to use their hands to make their junior love clubs look like they were sticking up). The girls and the other boys played coy on the sidelines.

Zel-da loved this game and was very good at it. Even though she was only five, she could simulate intercourse better than girls twice her age. She managed as usual to end up with ten-year-old Chee-cha, who had little budding breasts, and nine-year-old Kuka. Kuka, healthy young teeth bared in a proud grin, held the young Goddess up by the heels and dangled her in front of him while she played with him. Then all three of them rolled around on the ground enthusiastically until Zel-da delighted the entire company by concluding with an accurate imitation of the heated cries always forced from Oo-na, the timid Basket Weaving Lady, at the end.

Afterwards Zel-da wandered by herself into Gigla's hut for a nap. But while she was dreaming, a Demon must have gotten into her. On impulse Zel-da dug up the gourd Gigla kept hidden in a hole under the mat in the corner.

Zel-da was fully aware that the Dandruff of the Gods was sacred and taboo. However, she was a Goddess—even her brothers and sisters grudgingly conceded that. Peeking out the doorway to make sure no one was about, Zel-da balanced a little of the powder in the groove at the base of her thumb. Frowning in concentration (as a little girl will when she's being very careful not to spill) she sniffed the *epena* up her nose. Nothing happened. Hmph. She sniffed a little more.

Still nothing. Disappointed, she hid the gourd back in its hole and ran out into the sunlight.

The sunlight! Wham! Wham! She'd never seen anything like it. It was all different colors, and she could *hear* it. The Great Sun Himself was humming and buzzing at her like an enormous swarm of giant angry bees. Most unpleasant. Zel-da sucked in a lungful of buzzing air. "Aiyee!" she screamed.

Just then Gigla loomed up out of Nowhere and towered over her. She saw him peering at her eyes and at the traces of powder on her nose, and she knew he knew. Zel-da dropped to the ground, cringing and kissing Gigla's feet, begging him to save her.

Gigla, his life just one endless stream of one-thing-right-after-another, didn't know what the heck to do. He hurried Zel-da into his hut and began crooning to her, the way Banquo had taught him to croon to those few warriors who became overcome by the power of the powder during the Full Moon Ceremony sacred dances. Zel-da's terror turned to awe.

To Zel-da, whose critical faculties must have been seriously impaired by the drug, Gigla seemed to be singing with the voice of a wondrous God–the Jaguar God, to be specific. It was immensely powerful and yet so soothing. It was more than a voice; it was a Voice. And the Voice was speaking to her innermost self, deep calling to deep.

In a trance Zel-da rose to her feet. She seemed to be far, far away–beyond the skies, and beyond beyond the skies. She felt the vastness of the Great Jungle and the Oneness of All Things. She was filled with the power of her own people, Sun and Moon and Tree and Snake, all the Gods and Goddesses who lived, and, especially, loved, in the Heavens. Love. Love. That was the big light she'd seen when the whole village sang or danced together. That was the powerful force they brought into being. Zel-da, caught up in her Vision, began to twirl around outside the rude hut, to dance across the jungle floor.

The effect was very much heightened by the fact that Zel-da, in addition to her other special qualities, was also triple-jointed. She could bend her lissome young body into shapes that just weren't customary for humans. To Gigla and the slack-jawed tribal members nearby, it was obvious Zel-da was possessed by something rather impressive in the supernatural line. But by Whom or by What? "*That*," Gigla muttered to himself, "is the question."

When Zel-da finally slumped to the ground and curled up asleep, Gigla went out to face the music.

A council of all the men had already been called. The Chief summed the thing up in a nutshell. Zel-da had taken the sacred powder, and Zel-da was a female. These two failings, taken in conjunction, were punishable by death, with no possibility of appeal. On the other hand, Zel-da (at least so Gigla had said the day she arrived) was a Goddess. Perhaps the rules for Goddesses were different?

The Chief and the High Council voted to appoint Gigla a subcommittee-of-one to go out naked into the jungle, fast, flay himself, and do this and that, until the Gods revealed to him just what the heck They wanted done. Meeting adjourned.

It was now three days later. Gigla, after many a scary scrape with the local flora and fauna, still hadn't received an Answer from Above.

Just then there was a rustling along the path, and Gigla was startled to see a yellow-skinned, peculiar-eyed, fantastically garbed gentleman stumble into view. To Gigla he was obviously an adult God come to provide the Answer to the Little-Goddess Dilemma. He was actually a Japanese anthropologist from the expedition studying the tribe next door. And when Gigla took him back to the village, he recognized a prize when he saw one. Before anyone quite knew what happened, the Little Goddess was gone, and in her place lay a cheap pair of battered binoculars (see-from-far) and an assortment of canned goods (yum-eat-good).

Zel-da, age five, without having been consulted as to her own travel preferences, found herself hiking out of the stone age and jetting off to Kyoto.

Heavenly Hell

Zel-da received a full scholarship, as part of their much-talked-about "Pre-Schooler Involuntary Enrollment Program," from the famous (and once-Imperial) School for Mininuko Courtesans outside Kyoto.

When Kyoto was the seat of the Emperor (794-1868), the Mininuko School was attached to the Palace. If the Emperor or one of the high-ranking officials of the Court felt affairs of state pressing too heavily, he'd trudge through the convenient Heavenly Gates for some bright and graceful refreshment in the Flower and Willow World.

When the Emperor moved to Edo (Tokyo) in 1868, the Mininuko remained in Kyoto, at the insistence of the jealous Empress. The School resigned itself to a disastrous decline.

However, the disaster turned out to be one of those clouds with silver linings. In 1890 the Mininuko struck unexpected gold. One lucky August evening during the annual *Matsuage* (Fire Festival), the Abbot of a prestigious local monastery experienced a burning desire for female companionship. In deference to his spiritual status he was assigned, not to an ordinary Courtesan, but to Kineko, an accomplished *ichicko* or sorceress. Her specialty was revealing Divine Truths after entering a trance brought about by dancing.

The Abbot, too hot under the clerical collar to wait for the trance, pulled her in mid-dance onto the bed and almost immediately experienced an Orgasm of Light, which was felt by sensitives all over Japan. Word, as is its habit, immediately spread. If you wanted to achieve Enlightenment on your own, you meditated for years and years and years. If you preferred achieving the State of Bliss with a partner in an instant, you tried a certain Mininuko.

To cater to the new clientele, the Courtesans, under the direction of Kineko, plunged into Buddhist studies. Erotic spirituality became all the rage. Many of the Mininuko turned out to be quite good at it. Their track record surpassed the leading monasteries. A very small, but still encouraging, number of customers actually did find themselves filled with Light at the Moment of Truth.

By the time Zel-da arrived, the School was taking in two hundred or so five-and-six-year-olds each year, running them through a twelve-year training program (weeding rigorously along the way), and ending up each year with five or six new eighteen-year-olds, ready to take on any

Abbot or Abbess, Emperor or Empress, Prince or Princess on Earth. (For a very hefty fee. You wouldn't want to wander into the Mininuko Mansion unless your pants were simply bulging with yen.)

Zel-da, age five, found she'd been yanked from one of the most permissive and easygoing societies in the world and plunked down in one that was even more liberal, sexually, but infinitely more restrictive in most other ways. The little Goddess was *not* pleased.

Pa-Pa-Pa-Pa-Papa-San

Four mornings after her arrival, a hungry Zel-da sat stubbornly in her very own bedroom in the majestic Mininuko Mansion outside Kyoto. She was conducting a fast and meditation much more earnest than Gigla's recent effort.

She was impressed with Heaven; she wouldn't deny that. She loved (she'd be the first to admit) the magnificent hut, her clothes and her new "Goddess name" of Zelda Mishimoto. These things gave her, Zel-da felt, scope. And the wonders of bright steady light you just flicked on and off, pictures and voices and music coming from little boxes, hot and cold water that gushed out when you twisted that smooth-cold-hard thing–well, they'd never believe it back in the old village.

Other aspects of her new life, however, did not meet with this same unqualified approval. Take make-up for instance. Zel-da (or Zelda, now) felt you should deftly select all the brightest colors and then smear them liberally from head to foot. So festive! Her mentors favored a much more restrained approach. Hmph, how ridiculous.

Then there was the matter of how one went about the joy of communing with nature. Here, Zelda was an expert. You scampered naked out into the jungle, rolled happily in the dirt, ran after small things and away from large ones, and generally whooped and hollered and had a good time. In Heaven, however (or Kyoto, as it was called by the natives), they didn't even seem to have a jungle. It was absolutely uncivilized.

You simply wouldn't believe it. Zelda was actually expected to walk *slowly* around a minuscule "garden," being careful not to get her stiff and confining clothes dirty. Then she was supposed to sit and stare at some sterile rocks and a bunch of pitiful stunted bushes. When Zelda cavorted, they beat her with little switches–and no one seemed to think there was anything wrong in this. It was barbaric!

Well, you take a lively free-spirited jungle monkey, put it in a cage and whip it, and see what happens. Zelda was in the third day of a sit-down hunger strike that no one had been able to crack. There was a knock on the door, which Zelda ignored. Papa-san stuck his head in. "Ah, little one," he said.

Zelda turned to stare pointedly in the other direction. Papa-san took her by the hand.

"Come," he invited, tugging gently. "We dance."

There was something in Papa-san's tone which allowed Zelda to soften. She'd been putting up a brave front, but actually she was a very scared and lonely little girl. She missed Gigla. She missed the tribe. She missed being a Goddess among mortals. She missed being treated with unabashed love and respect and, yes, a little fear.

Here everyone babbled nonsense at her. Except for "Zelda," she couldn't understand a single word. Her sit-down strike was a cry for help more than anything else. Portly Papa-san understood this. He was very gentle as he smiled down at her. "Come," he repeated. "We dance."

Something inside Zelda said yes. Timidly, not understanding what the invitation meant, Zelda let herself be pulled to her feet. Papa-san walked over and put on a CD. He began clapping his hands and swaying happily in time to the music. After a few indecisive seconds Zelda began doing the same.

Papa-san attempted an intricate step. He looked so serious that Zelda giggled–almost the way she would have with Gigla. Papa-san broke into a grin. He giggled too. They capered around the room until Papa-san collapsed in the middle of the floor and Zelda plopped down on his ample tummy. In this strange place she'd found her first friend. He even let her play with his love club and seemed delighted at the sensations she could produce. At least this felt like home. Zelda decided it best to make do.

And make do she did. Much like she had plopped onto Papa-san's tummy, and with the same intensity as her hunger strike, she dove into her studies. Zelda was soon hard at work. Over the centuries the Mininuko had developed a number of unusual practices. Zelda majored in Languages, Dance, Martial Arts and the Erotic, in all of which she habitually received straight A's. "Knows Her Three Genitals" always had a gold star beside it on Zelda's report card. This subject was an especial favorite of the young Goddess-girl.

The Mininuko had identified three types of genitals–the male, the female and the round ones. The male genitals were those which became erect–the penis, the clitoris and the nipples. The female genitals were those which liked to be penetrated–the vagina, the mouth and the anus. The round (neutral) ones were the breasts and the testicles. Every standard human came equipped with at least one of all three types. And the Mininuko mastered all of them. A Mininuko could turn you from male to female to ambivalent and back with the flick of an eyelash. Zelda loved the complexity of the sexual games they played here; there was so much more range than the simple fun-fun she'd enjoyed with Kuka and the tribe-children.

But in some ways the strengths of the jungle never left her. When Zelda was determined to have her way, her delicate perfectly shaped nostrils flared, her startling violet eyes gleamed, her adorable and talented little foot started tapping, and nothing could move her, absolutely nothing. Papa-san swore that in his fifty years at the Mininuko Mansion, overseeing the training of thousand of young women in the art of pleasing Abbots and Emperors, he'd never seen anyone with half the promise of Zelda. But, by golly, he was also sure she was going to drive him to an early grave. Zelda just smiled her heart-stopping smile when he said this and kissed him pertly on the cheek.

Things proceeded swimmingly until Zelda was ten, when, early one morning, her best friend, Pretty Koko, ran in sobbing, "Manji is dead!" (Manji was the thirteen-year-old son of the head gardener.)

"What!?" Zelda gasped. "Manji!?"

"Dead! He committed *seppuku*."

"Oh!"

"*For you!*" Pretty Koko shrilled, horrified and thrilled.

"No!" Zelda screamed, stomach lurching. Her flirting and her subsequent refusal of his advances had just been a school lesson, playacting. Why had the game become terrible and real?

For a whole week Zelda wandered around in a daze, confusing genitals in class and even neglecting her daily vaginal calisthenics. Then she had a long talk with Papa-san and decided it was all right. It was only Death, and the Japanese have always admired ritual suicide. She realized Manji had done a brave and beautiful thing for her. She would revere his memory.

But this event opened a dark vein in Zelda's mind. She began fantasizing about killing herself with a boyfriend. She took to crooning *sonohachi* songs, those written in a style used only for relating stories of love suicide. She insisted that the class put on the famous love-suicide play *Kamiji*. Her performance in the female lead was so intense she frightened and electrified the audience. And as young Zelda immersed herself in Death, she became less thoughtlessly flirtatious and even more irresistible.

By the time Zelda was twelve, no still-beating male heart was safe. It was uncanny what Zelda could do with the tiniest flicker of an eye, the merest arch of an eyebrow, the barest curl of a lip. When it came time for her *mizu-age* (deflowering arrangement), Papa-san put an unusually high price on Zelda's maidenhead. But it was gladly met by an oil-rich Saudi Arabian Prince the day she turned thirteen.

Zelda's virginity was sold again to a South American dictator and then to a French diplomat, but these little deceptions are another story, and needn't concern us. The important point is that our young heroine blossomed ravishingly. And she loved sex. It felt so wonderful. It felt so right. She learned to give herself so freely, with such relish, such abandon, that her partner felt all-important and truly loved. She surrendered herself until her partner, too, surrendered, and then she guided him (or, occasionally, her) to a veritable garden of unearthly delights.

She was a Mininuko, and that was a very sacred thing. Her role, the task she'd solemnly accepted, was to provide love, to teach love, to *be* love to many people, to a few women and many men.

As one customer after another succumbed to her spell, word of this blossoming flower spread across the globe.

Zelda's Dilemma

As the balance of her days shifted from learning lessons to pleasing a paying clientele, Zelda's heart matured. She was glad she was placed where she could ease and soften hearts turned hard in the struggle for power, nudge men of consequence into bringing more love into the world.

She was proud she could reach into her clients and entice forth all that was best in them. Subtly, ever so subtly, dredging up the good she knew was buried in them, she led them in the direction of merging their great worldly power with true love from the heart. She was pleased to watch the pale halo of light around her clients change as she loved them, from selfish and frightened and angry colors, from muddy browns and grays, to warm and open and loving colors, to pink and royal purple, and maybe even on to radiant white.

Zelda was doing the work for which she was meant. She was making a difference in the world. Why, on a couple of occasions, she'd actually prevented wars. She was a one-courtesan United Nations. And on the night of her Dance debut, the evening that Baron Fred had first seen her onstage, she'd been able to love a whole group, one after the other. She'd had a glimpse of being able to love them all at once. Life was perfect.

If only…no, her life was perfect, a Mininuko shouldn't wish for such things. But if only… well, if only she could not just love, but fall in love. The men in the audience that night, the ones she'd be sleeping with for the next few months, if only so many of them weren't so unattractive and so old. She'd have appreciated a more…balanced mix. Papa-san watched her so closely she never got to meet any boys her own age.

The very afternoon after her debut, while her maid, Honako, was helping her dress, Zelda chanced upon a Tokyo gymnastics meet on tv. A team from the United States was competing. A blond on the parallel bars set her heart spinning.

"Oh!" Zelda gasped. "Who's that angel?!" She could feel herself dancing with him, wrapping herself naked around him. Could she meet him? No, Papa-san would never let her sleep with someone who couldn't afford her rates. It just couldn't be worked.

Or could it? Maybe lively Pretty Koko could think of something. If anyone could get around the rules, she could. Oh, she must show him to Pretty Koko!

"Quick, quick!" she urged Honako. "Bring Pretty Koko to me. Hurry!"

"Oh!" her maid squeaked.

"Hurry!" Zelda insisted, but Honako just stood there wringing her hands.

"You have not heard?" Honako inquired timidly.

"Heard? Heard what?"

"Pretty Koko has had...an accident."

"What!?" Zelda tore from her suite and raced to Pretty Koko's room. The ninja Nissan was on guard. Foolishly he tried to stop her. Five seconds later, ignoring his moans, Zelda stepped over him and burst through the door.

"Pretty Koko!" she gasped. "What happened?!" Her friend's head was wrapped in bandages.

"I tried to run away," Pretty Koko whispered weakly.

"But what happened to you?"

"The ninja tracked me down. They tied me...to a post and...threw acid in my face."

"Oh no! Who did it? Papa-san will punish them!"

"Papa-san was there. Papa-san ordered...it. He said I had been naughty...one time too often. He said I would be an...object lesson to the other girls. He said...from now on...with my new face...I could cater to the...specialty trade."

Zelda felt her world crumbling. She fled to her room.

"Pretty Koko," she cried brokenly into her pillow, and then, realizing the even greater tragedy, "Papa-san. My father!"

Yes, Papa-san had been her father, her cheerful benevolent adopted father. She'd never suspected him of having such a ruthless, brutal, non-Mininuko side.

After the first rush of hurt and hatred had subsided, she decided to make sure he was as bad as she thought. The first time she was alone with him after Pretty Koko's capture, she asked, in her usual straightforward manner, "Would you do something like that to me if I tried to run away?"

A look of pain stole into Papa-san's eyes. "Ah, my lotus flower," he sighed. "I wouldn't spoil your beauty, but I would have to punish you. It would be very painful for me, very painful indeed."

Zelda excused herself and returned to her own apartment, where she knelt down in front of her shrine, shut her eyes, looked inside and watched her trust and her innocence die.

Papa-san had meant it as a compliment, telling her he loved her so much the decision to punish her would be difficult. Zelda saw a different truth. Papa-san loved her so little he would force her to stay here against her will. Papa-san wasn't a true Mininuko at all. Money and power were more important to him than love was, than she was. She wasn't his daughter; she was just a favorite employee. No, a favorite slave.

As it slowly withered and died, she could see how exquisite, how fragile, how precious was the love and trust Papa-san had chosen to forfeit. She thanked him for revealing this beauty even as she mourned its loss. And she began plotting her escape. Six weeks later...

A Baroness Nails Down a Contortionist

"Damn!" Ethel swore to herself as she squirmed on the priceless-but-uncomfortable Louis XIV chair in the elegant Rothschild salon. "Damn, damn, damn, damn, damn!"

She was in a quandary. Fred's odd confusion when she'd asked him about his Japanese computer conference had led her to hire a discreet private investigator. So she now knew all about her soulmate's extramarital excursion to the Mininuko Cat House.

She'd also noted Fred's peculiar enthusiasm for this Rothschild shindig, and his bumbling attempts to persuade her not to come. But it wasn't until the two hundred guests had been herded into the salon and the surprise entertainment announced that she'd put two and two together.

She'd still thought the affair could be easily handled. But now Zelda was gliding seductively onstage, and the first glimpse of her rival drove a shaft straight through Ethel's ample breast. As did the sight of her mate, gaping at Zelda with the sort of adoring look Sir Lancelot might have directed at Guinevere, had she also happened to be holding the Holy Grail. Fred had never strayed before. What should she do?

And as if matters weren't already complicated enough, Ethel's nipples suddenly turned positively electric. Her Gift had to choose that precise moment to shout, "Eureka! She's the one!" Ethel knew, beyond all doubt, that Zelda was the only possible choice for her big movie's Mystery Juliet. Damn! Damn, damn, damn, damn, damn!

And Zelda was sensational! Against her will Ethel found herself caught up, enraptured, by Zelda's graceful hypnotic movements across the tiny stage. This was a naked erotic dance which left the entire audience, Ethel included, tingling.

Afterwards their host presented Zelda and Papa-san to the von Elms. Ethel decided to pretend nothing was amiss.

"Honey, that was quite a dance," she gushed. "I swear you must be made of rubber."

The Baron Frederick contented himself with stammering, "H-h-how d-do you d-do?" and trying not to stare at Zelda.

"*What can I do?*" Fred was agonizing to himself. "*How can I get rid of Ethel?*" He must have this night with Zelda! He *must!*

Zelda wasn't sure why tonight's client was with his wife; so she confined herself to purring, "I'm so pleased to see you, Baron." Fred was immensely relieved she didn't add "again."

"Hmm," Zelda thought, "a little lazy, this one. A turtle. He hides in his nice cozy shell and lets his wife deal with the world. But great capacity for good, if handled properly." Yes, Zelda had a good fix on the Baron. But what about this famous wife? Was she to join them? She turned to Ethel.

"And, Baroness…" She trailed off. My goodness! The intense colors, the strength in this woman! And the love! And the anger and hurt!

There was only one thing to do. She fixed Ethel with her most sincere and penetrating gaze and silently made to her the Mininuko Pledge: "Yes, I could truly love you. Yes, I do truly love you. Love is All."

Ethel, her heart thumping and her head awhirl, blurted out, "Come with me!" and drew the little quartet into a small sitting room. Thank God she retained enough presence of mind not to blurt out her offer in public. She turned to Zelda.

"My Juliet! You are my Juliet!" Ethel declared. "You have to star in my movie!"

Creativity was running amok in the Baroness. Her nipples were making her practically squirm. "We'll make Juliet a dancer, of course," she burbled. "Your performance just has to be seen by millions. Not millions, billions. Your gift should be shared with the world."

Ethel had poked precisely the right nerve. She'd struck Zelda's secret yen. If her work as a Thousand-Petal Courtesan hadn't made it impossible, Zelda would have loved to thrill vast audiences. She couldn't agree with the Baroness more.

"Perhaps Papa-san would consider it," Zelda suggested demurely, her voice tinkling like little bells.

Papa-san, meanwhile, was busy comparing Zelda's going rate as a courtesan known to the select few to what her going rate would be as a courtesan desired by the whole world. There had been talk of the Mininuko playing a more visible role on the international scene. Yes, there were decided possibilities.

"What would my lotus flower earn?" Papa-san wondered casually.

"Twenty million plus points," the Baroness replied, equally casually. She wanted all the publicity a huge salary to an unknown would bring.

"Dollars U.S.?" Papa-san gasped.

"Dollars U.S.," Ethel affirmed.

"It might be possible," Papa-san admitted.

Zelda was liking the idea more and more. A few innocent questions gleaned the information that she'd be in California, out from under Papa-san's eagle eye, for several months. Papa-san, of course, would expect her to return, value greatly enhanced, to her old work when the film was completed. Zelda didn't know what she'd do when the movie was finished. One thing she did know, however. She was determined not to return to Kyoto. "It will be enjoyable, yes?" she asked.

"Oh, sugar, it'll be a ball!" Ethel assured her. "You think about it. Well, come on, Fred. I'm exhausted. Let's go to bed."

To win a wife, Baron Frederick had once defied his father in private. He found he simply couldn't manage to defy this same wife in public. With one last helpless lingering glance, like Moses denied the Promised Land, Freddikins allowed himself to be led away.

"At least," Fred consoled himself, "Ethel doesn't suspect a thing."

The Plot Thickens
Fifi Gets Flustered and Bustered

Watching the Baroness Ethelina usher Jason into the von Elm's Bev Hills drawing room, Fifi was reminded of Moses sauntering down off Sinai and proudly presenting the Tablets to the Tribes. (Fifi wasn't an actual witness, of course. She'd have been a mere child at the time.)

"Fifi, meet Jason. Jason, this is Fifi," Ethel, mistress of understatement, announced. "And, I declare, I don't know which of you I envy more. You're both in for a real treat!"

Fifi didn't doubt the Baroness for an instant. "An Angel!" Fifi cried to herself, "with a decidedly capital 'A.'"

Fifi, to her uncertain knowledge, had never even thought in terms of capital-"A" Angels, but she was definitely thinking in terms of them now. And young Greek gods and Prince Charmings too.

She took it even further than that. You know, Fifi didn't know why it was–Lord knows the physical resemblance was minimal at best–but for some reason Jason reminded her of Bo-ku. She didn't know what it was, but something about Jason was Bo to the life.

Jason's reaction (or, rather, Buster's reaction) was, to Ethel's surprise, also enthusiastic. Buster was exulting, "Hoo, baby, those hands! Sense those suckers shimmer! Ecstasy! Put those talented things on me! Woo woo!" And Jason always trusted Buster, so he greeted Fifi with one of his trademarked melting grins.

It went through Fifi like a dose of salts. "This way," Fifi invited dazedly, starting to lead her heavenly gentleman to the guest bedroom where her massage table was lurking. Then she was distracted by the firm young hand gripping hers. Ooh, this Angel was decidedly made of oh-so-silky flesh, and she was going to massage him.

Oops, unless she was having another…Oh darn! Oh dear! Fifi could feel she was flushing, and her breathing sounded as though she'd slipped her fan belt. "Please," she prayed, "don't let this be a heart attack!

"Anything!" Fifi begged. "Just not now! Give me an hour even! Just don't let it be an attack right now!"

Jason, hardly able to miss Fifi's distress, almost yelped for Ethel, but instead he reached out a steadying hand to Fifi. "Are you all right?" he asked anxiously.

The Angel Gabriel, Jr. was concerned for her welfare. Fifi felt herself coming back into control. "Thank you, dear," she wheezed. "Yes, I'm just fine. Oop! Whup! Here we are."

She stumbled into the bedroom and made for her big comfy chair. "Just give me a moment," she panted. "Go ahead, dear. You climb onto the massage table."

Fifi was startled by a brief flash of color. This turned out to be Jason's bright-red, fresh-smelling, "Jockey brand" briefs, which were being exuberantly flung by their owner to join the rest of his raiment on the rug. Well, he *was* a quick little bunny, wasn't he? And if he wanted to be nude, why not?

Fifi felt a sudden surge of energy. "What's the problem you've been having?" she asked her new patient brightly. Jason explained about his "low-impact ejaculations."

Orgasms almost without touching! Why, that was very similar to her own problem, but from the other person's point of view. How interesting! And oh my! Bobbing its rosy head at her from Jason's "convenient central location" was a truly heart-stopping family-size primary reproductive organ–an organ which, could it but speak, would obviously be on the very verge of panting, "Woof, woof!"

"Glory be!" Fifi breathed, rolling her eyes heavenward. "An Angel of Love!" She felt a little tingle tentatively starting up in her nether regions.

"Good Lord!" Fifi gurgled to herself, "I thought those nerves all quit firing years ago!"

The whole situation was so staggering a lesser eighty-something would have promptly succumbed to a stroke of terror and/or ecstasy. Even Fifi, seasoned trouper that she was, found her breathing again becoming a trifle erratic. And wasn't that a tasteful gallon or two of extra blood pounding merrily through her ears?

"Settle down, Fifi," she admonished herself.

Oops, if it wasn't one thing, it was three more. Without warning, the chronic tic in Fifi's left cheek began twitching like crazy, making her whole left hip tingle. Fearing her shaky old pins would no longer hold her, Fifi lurched towards the massage table for support.

"You OK?" Jason asked, a look of concern on his face.

"Oh yes. I just got a little twitch in my leg."

Jason, divining the real cause of Fifi's perturbation, grinned. A lesser eighteen-year-old would have hastened to explain, "Oh, I always get a hard-on when I get naked." Jason just pointed out to Fifi, "I think Buster likes you."

"Buster?" Fifi looked around the room.

Jason looked down and said, "Buster, meet Fifi. Fifi, meet Buster."

"Ooh!" Fifi tittered, like an eighty-something schoolgirl. She even started to blush.

Jason smiled. With the formalities out of the way, he sighed and returned to his back, legs spread apart and hands over his head. He wriggled like a healthy puppy into the most comfortable position. Buster seemed to be bobbing up and down hoping for a puppy biscuit.

Between the hard reality of Buster, and the lingering scent of Bo-ku, Fifi had an inspiration. On impulse, she decided to give Jason a real massage–to rub his body as well as wave her hands over him. After sixty years of being afraid to touch her patients, the dam finally burst.

"All right." Fifi took three big breaths and let them out. "Here goes."

She began by placing her fingers gently on Jason's chest and then running them lightly over his whole body–just to get a feel for him, to get an idea of the lay of the land. Oh, those smooth muscles! Ahhh, that perfect honey skin!

"Mmmm!" Jason sighed. He'd been having people massage him since he was a little boy, and he could tell instantly that Fifi was a natural. Her fingers *knew*.

Fifi's nervousness disappeared. First she concentrated on Jason's muscles. She started at his shoulders, worked down and up both arms and then kneaded her way down his chest to his waist. She couldn't apply as much pressure as she once could, but she found she didn't really have to push very hard at all. Jason wasn't tensing against her, and, anyway, her fingers just seemed to bypass the brain and whisper directly to the muscles, "Relax." Jason was the answer to a masseuse's prayer, a client who "really got into it," who *appreciated* her lifetime of skills, just *surrendered* to her.

Fifi worked away. Her gentle exploratory touch would find the tension. She'd soothe a little, and Jason would just allow it to drain away. Yes, ooh, ahhh. Now the next spot. There. Yes. Ooh. Yes, ooh, ahhh.

What a team they were. Already they were both breathing deeply and in synch. He was really letting her in. She could get right through to his deeper muscles.

Ah, she was past the surface and was feeling Jason himself. Fifi felt a warm pinkish radiance seeping in and filling the chambers of her battered old heart as she moved down and massaged Jason's legs.

Jason was pretty much Jello by now, while Buster was solid as the Rock of Gibraltar. As extremely horny young people will, Jason was raising his buttocks up and squirming. It was time to work on his special problem. Fifi could just tell Buster had a hair-trigger. She stretched out her hand. Nice Buster.

Down, Boy!

Fifi was ready to start on Jason's chakras and premature congratulations. She used her left hand to lift up Jason's testicles so she could cup her right hand underneath, on his first chakra.

"Oh!" Jason thought to himself, as well he might. It was impossible to describe, but no one had ever dealt with Buster's balls quite as casually and expertly as Fifi was dealing with them now.

Fifi's hand was calm, and it wasn't trying to arouse Buster. Fifi was focused on a spot Jason hadn't really noticed before. She was right over this intense warm place below his testicles, and she was producing the most peculiar and pleasant sensations.

Not that Fifi was unaware of Buster. In some indefinable way Jason could feel the warmth and electricity from Fifi's hand somehow filling Buster all the way out to the tip. And Fifi's hand seemed to be regarding Buster, the way a top photographer would critically eye a model, or an expert breeder might assess a thoroughbred stallion.

And indeed Fifi's hand was doing just that. "Lovely!" her hand was enthusing. "Buster, you're so handsome! But what's this I feel? This sort of overcharged feeling?"

What could Fifi do to correct Buster's problem? Well, she'd do an overall balancing first. Fifi's plan was to connect, one by one, all his chakras with each other, letting the two separate energies merge and support one another.

Keeping her right hand in place, Fifi cupped her left hand over the top of Jason's head. This was his crown chakra, the thousand-petal lotus, the baby's soft spot, the point at which the soul floats (hopefully gracefully) out of the body at death. When the crown chakra fully opened, Pure White Light would stream in and do simply marvelous things. Yes, she could feel it.

And so could Jason. He could feel a current all the way down his spine. Wow! This Fifi was a magician. He felt like Young Arthur being massaged by Granny Merlin. But he was also strangely at peace. With Fifi's hands cupping his head and his groin, he felt as though he were lying safe in a cradle or a womb.

Fifi moved her left hand down to the center of Jason's forehead, to the fabled "third eye" through which we peek into other dimensions. Jason felt/saw colored lights inside his head. He felt as though he could float right off the table.

Fifi moved her left hand down to the fifth chakra at the base of Jason's throat, the source of creativity and expression, of what he'd been "born to say." Jason knew he was in the hands of a Healer. He arched his head back to expose more of his throat, making a contented purring sound.

Fifi moved her left hand down to the fourth, or heart, chakra in the center of Jason's chest. Here was pure unselfish love. Here was confidence that the Universe *was* Love, and death no more than a marvelous transition. Fifi, eyes closed, began forgetting her wrinkled old exterior. The true Fifi, the delightfully ageless young woman, began to emerge. Jason felt himself filled with warm pink light. This was beyond words.

Fifi moved her left hand down to the third, or power, chakra above Jason's navel. Mmm, Jason felt strength and balance. His body centered into truer and deeper alignment. He also was starting to feel even more erotic. Much more erotic.

Fifi moved her left hand down to Jason's second, or sex, chakra, below his navel. Here was Nature's Strongest Force and Most Whimsical Gift, the irresistible urge to merge.

Fifi felt an incredible surge of pleasure. She'd have to draw her hand away to a little safer… My goodness! Oh dear!

"Arrugh!" Jason groaned, indicating by thrusts and gyrations that Fifi could make him very happy by moving her right hand just a little bit north or her left hand a little bit south. He was getting glimpses of what sex could be, of what love could be.

Those hands! With his eyes closed, all at once Jason realized something. These weren't the hands of an old crone!

That Ethel! She'd set this all up. She'd had Fifi slip away and his Mystery Juliet take her place! He started to open his eyes and then thought, "Nope, I want to get to know her this way first."

· · ·

Fifi felt young again, but she was no longer the awkward neophyte. She had the hands of a skilled masseuse. Everything was so…What was she…Oh yes, she was working on an Angel's sex chakra.

And she was going to make love with him. Oh, Lordy, was she ever going to make love with him, just as soon as she figured out how to correct this overcharge in his second chakra.

· · ·

Jason was floating, and his Mystery Juliet, whom Ethel had chosen as the most beautiful woman in the world, was an inch away from making love with him…

· · ·

Jason's first and second chakras were Fifi's entire Universe. She rode with them, soothing and molding the energy. Ah, there was the trouble. If she just sort of…

· · ·

Ordinarily Buster would have spurted long ago. The tiniest touch would have done it. But Princess Charming, maddeningly, hadn't touched him. Jason had been thrusting his hips and making love to thin air. He was pent up to the point of frenzy. He couldn't stand it anymore.

Jason wrapped his arms around Princess Charming. He pulled her onto the table with him.

. . .

"Erp!" young Fifi squeaked as Jason succeeded in rendering her entirely innocent of clothing. Her eyes flew open, and she caught sight of a liver-spotted old hand.

"Wha'?" Fifi gasped. "Oh no! I'm not eighteen!"

And things were going much too fast. If they were going to have actual sex, Jason should be gradually *eased* into the sight her body–of what jovial Ethel termed "the remains." As soon as he caught sight of her nakedness, Jason's ardor would cool. Fifi resigned herself to saying cheerfully, "Oh, that's all right, Jason. Perhaps some other time."

But, wonder of wonders, Jason wasn't repulsed! (Luckily he seemed to have his eyes closed.) Instead, he was enfolding her in his silken arms and pressing her tightly against his highly developed pectoral muscles. Paradise!

But, wait a minute! Jason was squeezing her much too tightly! She was being crushed!

"Yeep!" screeched Fifi, starting to struggle. This was no joke. In another minute her frail old bones would begin snapping like popcorn.

And, *yeow*, without an ounce of preparation or prevention, Jason was attempting to sail (or, rather, *thrust*) his destroyer-class love boat right through the rusty locks of her moss-covered old love canal. This was awful.

"FIFI FULBRIGHT BO-KU, 84, RAPED BY OLYMPIC GYMNAST, 18." Even the thought of this marvelous obituary provided Fifi with only a fleeting instant of comfort.

Fifi had always secretly believed that when push came to shove, she'd turn out to be every bit as nonviolent as Gandhi, as Nelson Mandela, as Martin Luther King. Sadly, such did not prove the case. Now that she was actually in danger of her very life, Fifi tossed her pacifist principles to the winds. She made a desperate lunge, fully prepared to grab Jason's love potatoes and MASH!

Jason was reaching desperately for Nirvana. Fifi was battling both arthritis and the habits of a lifetime to get her gnarled old fingers to tighten in the grip which would send Jason screeching into the soprano section.

Just before she could get her reluctant digits to execute a painful clutch, Jason, with a full-throated, "EEEEEEYAHAAAAAA!" spilled (or, rather, flung) his seed liberally over the massage table, the rug, a certain astonished senior citizen and himself.

"ARRNGH!" Jason ejaculated, sinking back onto the massage table.

"GRRNPH," he clarified.

"Shwoosh!" Fifi exclaimed. She was shaking and gasping for breath. Sixty years a masseuse, and she'd never come this close to being, well, raped. And by an Angel! It was all too heartbreaking and confusing. Fifi's trembling grew worse, and she started to sob. With that, her heart went over the edge.

Fifi Experiences Her First Death

"Unh," Fifi groaned. She'd had several "little attacks," and she'd been hard put to enjoy them. They'd been just awful, but they'd been nothing compared to this.

Fifi's extremities were going numb, even as they continued flailing uncontrollably. "Unnnhh!!" she protested in panic. An enormous pain knifed through her, the worst thing she'd ever felt in her life.

The next thing Fifi knew, she was floating up near the ceiling, watching Jason staring, aghast, at her lifeless form. Her cataracts were gone, she noted. She was seeing clearly for the first time in years. She tried to reach down, tap Jason on the shoulder and assure him she was all right, but her hand went right through him. You can probably guess what came next.

Fifi found herself traveling at great speed through a long tunnel. She came out in a wondrous place filled with Beings of Light. Old friends were there, and a Guide, who reviewed her life with her. It wasn't the big events that seemed to matter. It was the little incidents where she'd learned something about the way the world works or where she'd shown love or failed to show it. Knowledge and Love, the Guide showed her, were the only things that really mattered in life. They were the only things you could "take with you."

Then the Guide took her back to a specific day when she was five years old, playing "doctor" with little Rupert. Fifi heard her Mother screaming, "FIFI! HOW COULD YOU?!"

She remembered the wonderful feeling she'd had just before her Mother had started shrieking at her. She saw God being, not angry, but disappointed, that His Greatest Gift, the tingly portions, were regarded as evil and nasty, when they were actually the most beautiful things in the world.

"You have some more living to do, Fifi," the Guide told her, as she absorbed what she'd just learned. "You still have something to do that is going to be a Teaching, a Service, to the human race."

"Wha'…what do you mean?" Fifi asked.

"You'll see," he assured her Lovingly. "It's time to go back now. Be content. You've lived your life well. I salute the Divinity within you."

As Fifi re-entered her body, she felt an incredible surge of love and pleasure, and had her very first shimmering orgasm. She emerged looking and feeling ten years younger.

As he saw her open her eyes, Jason laid his hand over hers. "God," he said, "I've never done anything like that before. I'm really sorry."

Lordy, Fifi sighed, *he is a beauty. And, speaking of understatement, virile to a fault.* Aloud she assured him, "Don't give it another thought. I feel wonderful!"

And he actually thinks I'm attractive! she continued to herself. *I mean, he must. He couldn't resist me.*

Over the odd half century Fifi had watched herself change from a plain young lady into a withered old crone. And yet Jason had gotten turned on at the very sight of her, *before* the massage.

It was such a relief to find a young man who actually found her physically attractive, just as she was. How long had it been since she'd been able to feel alluring? Never, perhaps? Fifi didn't even want to think. Maybe she should suggest to Jason that they try again tomorrow.

Yes! That would prove there were no hard feelings. Why, Christian charity practically demanded it. But, oops, what if he attacked her again?

Better not, Fifi reluctantly concluded. It would be safer just to let Jason drift right on out of her life.

Jason put his arm around Fifi's shoulder to comfort her, and Fifi felt her pinched old nostrils being positively invaded by the heady squeaky-clean scent of youth. The cautious resolution she'd just made fell by the wayside.

I'm in love, Fifi realized in astonishment. *For the first time since Bo died, I'm truly in love.* Her battered old heart soared. *With a man who'll probably kill me*, she realized with chagrin. Her battered old heart plummeted.

Oh, quit torturing yourself, Fifi, she admonished the Romantic within. *You can't see Jason again. It would just be too risky.*

Jason, meanwhile, was musing, *Up until I lost control, that was the most amazing thing that's ever happened to me. I'll ask Fifi if we can try again.*

Then he, too, had second thoughts. *No, I scared her too much. She wouldn't want to see me again after what I did tonight.*

Then an even darker thought blackened his normally cheery brain. *And what if I did it again!? I can't trust myself not to space out and lose control. I almost killed her this time. I'd better just keep my mouth shut.*

And so they parted. Jason tried to forget Fifi by concentrating on preparing for the Olympics. Fifi tried to forget Jason by plunging back into work, where she blossomed.

Fifi and I Tag-Team Death and Get Arrested for Murder AND Prostitution

Jason hightailed back to the Midwest as soon as he'd cleaned up from his most dangerous massage with Fifi. Drat! I'd have to get my hands on him another time.

Over the next few days, Fifi and I actually got to know each other, and found we had much in common. After her near-death experience with Jason, she decided it would be safer to follow Aunt Ethel's suggestion and tag-team with me. The next afternoon Aunt Ethel sent us our first client.

Fifi and I were in the guest bedroom with the massage table when there was a knock at the door. Who's today's hottest screen siren? Exactly. That's who walked in. I was delighted, but Fifi was a little puzzled, since she was used to working on people who had something wrong with them.

No matter. Our client undressed and lay face down on the table, and Fifi and I began. I started physically rubbing, while Fifi commenced guiding energy through our temptress's body. I was feeling energy too, the way I did with the one-in-a-hundred. When our client turned over I asked, "Do you want your tingly portions included or excluded?" I'd found that was the best way to do it. "May I include your tingly portions?" made it a rejection of me if they said no. This way they were free to choose what they actually wanted, and then I'd adjust to their decision.

Fifi, however, was shocked. Buster excepted, tingly portions were a definite no-no. But our client said, "Included, please," and Fifi evidently decided, hell, you're only old once, because she didn't say anything.

Fifi cupped chakras, and I rubbed skin, including the erogenous zones as I encountered them, until at the end I began really concentrating on our client's honeypot, with Fifi's hand cupped over mine. Our client had a truly spectacular orgasm, and left declaring that she felt wonderful.

Before dinner I thought I'd better pay a couple of credit cards, and smiled at how convenient it was that hundreds of miles from home I could go online and get my balances and then log on to my bank account to make the payments. When I did so I got a big surprise. There was an extra $10,000 in my account.

I mentioned it at dinner, and Ethel said, "Oh yes, I'm charging $14,000 a session for you and Fifi, and your client tipped $6,000."

"What!"

"Is that all right?"

"Well, yes. My God!"

"You're welcome."

And thus it was that Fifi and I began peddling capital-"O" Orgasms to the world's top sexpots. HALF MY THIRD WISH, FILLING MY BED WITH MOVIE STARS, HAD ALREADY COME TRUE! As long as Fifi and I didn't have sex with each other, I decided this set-up was just peachy.

Fifi adjusted admirably to her new circumstances. At age 84, she became Hollywood's hottest hooker—such a scandal-waiting-to-happen that Ethel secretly signed her as Juliet's Attendant in her big upcoming movie.

Fifi and I were great as a team. I could feel energy flowing as a strong current, rather than a subtle emanation. We both knew instinctively just when, where and what to do. It was so much fun to supernova movie stars!

Despite all the fun, Fifi was still spooked by nearly dying. At her suggestion, we began to alternate our paying sessions with volunteer freebies at local hospices. She wanted to learn more about the Great Transition. Pretty wise for an 84-year-old with so much mileage, I thought.

Our first double date with death was hosted by a beautiful young man named Frank. He was down to skin and bones, but he was so sweet, and so grateful that Fifi and I were massaging him. When we met him, he could barely whisper. His eyes seemed mostly fixed in wonder on a point somewhere beyond us. He was more sensitive to energy than any of our movie star clients.

Although he hadn't had an erection in over a year, Frank asked us to include his genitals. Including them, of course, was absolutely against the hospice rules, but since he had a private room, we could accommodate him without the staff knowing. While Fifi was massaging his legs, I remember putting my left hand on the crown chakra on top of his head and gently cupping his genitals with my right. A big smile spread across his face. I moved my right hand on down to cup his first chakra, and then it happened. I have the strongest impression that Frank *chose* that moment to die, that he, not Fifi or I, was responsible for what happened in the next few moments. I think he *drew* a bolt of white lightning down through the top of my head, out my right hand and up his spine. A huge black abyss opened before me. There was a rush of wind, then a jolt of sheer ecstasy. When I returned to my senses, I found that Frank, Fifi and I had all ejaculated, and Frank was dead.

There was a sacred feeling in the hushed room. I shut my eyes and asked Ash-Kar about what had happened.

"Death can be highly erotic," a deep, reverent voice advised me. "For you and the person dying as well. At the moment of death there can be an enormous longing and appreciation for the physical."

For the next two people who died under our hands, nothing special seemed to happen. No lightning, no wind. They just slipped away.

The third one was Charlie. The nurse said she thought he was very close. He'd been asking for a massage, though; so I sat down beside him on the bed, introduced Fifi and me and asked if he still wanted a rub. He nodded his head and croaked out, "Please." When I asked whether he wanted his genitals included or excluded, he gasped, "Included."

Again, he was someone extremely sensitive to energy. And I could put my hands on any two spots on his body and *feel* the electricity zinging between them. We reached what I think was the instant of Death. Although I'd never heard one before, I think he was starting a death rattle. It sent scary shivers right through me.

I didn't feel a bolt of white lightning entering through the top of my head. Instead, I felt white light simply welling up inside me. Then I felt myself being lifted up on a giant ocean wave. I gasped. Next thing I knew, I was sitting on Charlie's bed with that wonderful sharp clear feeling, and Fifi was swaying gracefully over us. None of us had ejaculated, and Charlie wasn't dead. He was sleeping peacefully.

Within a week he was able to get up and go to the bathroom by himself. Within two weeks he was able to leave the hospice. He was convinced the massage had cured him.

Fifi and I continued working with the critically ill for months. Sometimes they died spectacularly, "going out with a bang," as Ethel put it. Sometimes they just slipped away. And five of them apparently cured themselves.

I can't describe how peculiar it is to enjoy a shimmering orgasm with someone famous and gorgeous and in perfect health, and then enjoying an orgasm with someone incredibly frail and at death's door. The two experiences are as alike and as different as they can be.

Our experiments came crashing to a halt when Fifi and I became the first grandma/grandson healing team to be arrested for prostitution and murder through orgasm. The murder charge was quickly dropped. We may actually have slightly hastened the deaths of some of our terminal patients, but it would be very hard to prove—and there were the five people willing to testify that we'd saved their lives.

On the prostitution charge, Ethel's lawyers took a novel approach. Sure, we included our clients' genitals. We enjoyed the sexual aspects of our services at least as much as our clients did. We weren't grudgingly providing sex for money. We were doing it out of love and for our own sheer enjoyment. If they had a willing movie star under their fingers, who could resist, and why should they? The pursuit of happiness. That was the contention.

Then these legal eagles pointed out the Constitution provided for separation of the views of religion from the laws of the state. Well, Joy was our religion. Sexual touch was our sacrament. And anyone was allowed to make donations to support the cause.

Believe it or not, a mere two months before the Meeting of Romeo and Juliet and Crystal

Palace Warming, the jury agreed the state could not require citizens to view portions of their own bodies as ugly, evil, vile, disgusting and not to be loved or touched...either during a "religious service" or a business transaction.

Fifi and I were freed in a frenzy of priceless publicity. Ethel, no fool, quietly added me to the film as Romeo's Attendant.

"Just imagine the riot, Cowpossums, when you're introduced at the party. You two come out onstage, the guests go wild, you're beamed to screens worldwide by the satellite feed...why, my nips are positively ecstatic just thinking about it!"

Jason and I Become Buds

Aunt Ethel got Fifi out of the mansion one afternoon and brought Jason back so I could have a try at fixing his amusing sexual problem. I, of course, was completely smitten, and really wanted to help him tame Buster. It was a fight to the finish.

After I'd massaged the rest of Jason it was time to tackle Buster. I told Jason to tell me when I was getting too close, and he stopped me a couple of inches away. I tried approaching down from Jason's stomach and up from his thighs, but couldn't get too close. Then I remembered my Ash-Kar dream with Horass the hippo and how he waved protuberances with the most sensitive membrane in the Universe. I remembered what it had been like in the dream and applied it to approaching Buster. Eventually, very slowly, very, very carefully, I was able actually to grasp Buster and hold him while keeping my hand completely still. I was disappointed it only lasted for about thirty seconds before Buster exploded, but Jason was ecstatic.

Always before, he'd have a nanosecond of being on the verge, and then he'd erupt, but this time he was on the very verge for a full thirty seconds, and it felt wonderful. He raved to Aunt Ethel that we were making progress, so she shipped me back to the Midwest with him. He'd come to my hotel suite every night for sessions.

To my surprise we had a lot to talk about. He had a lively sense of humor and liked zingers as much as I did. Also he was interested in figuring out how society could quit being so uptight about nudity and do more cuddling.

His sexual problem was fascinating, but we couldn't quite solve it. On the physical side, if I was really, really careful, sometimes I could slowly move closer and even hold Buster awhile. But as soon as I moved my hand just a little bit, Jason would explode. As far as energy goes, I'd try cupping different pairs of chakras and trying to sense what needed to be changed, but didn't have too much luck. We became the best of friends, but didn't solve his problem.

Ethel Pops the Question. Sight Unseen, Jason and Zelda are Engaged!

At first, Ethel had kept Jason out of the media. Then, at the Summer Olympics, Jason won five gold medals; and the world became enraptured! Within a week he had millions in endorsement deals, and the name "Buster" splashed happily across the international mediascape. Since the paparazzi had seen Jason coming and going from the von Elm estate on several occasions, there was plenty of speculation that he might be the Mystery Romeo–rumors that Ethel would neither confirm nor deny. She did, however, have a brainstorm. One afternoon by her pool Ethel was struck by a notion so immense she flopped back in her recliner and worked her mouth like an asthmatic butterfish. "What if they got *married!*?" she spluttered to Fred.

"What if who got married?" Fred wanted to know.

"The Mystery Romeo and Juliet! People are expecting to see two actors playing a role. What if it weren't just a movie, but a real wedding ceremony? Two gorgeous strangers, meeting for the first time to get married. That'd be news!"

"But would Zelda and what's-his-name want to do it?" Fred asked–hoping fervently that the answer was no. Zelda still took up most of his fantasies. He didn't want her to marry someone else.

"You've never seen me propose," Ethel answered determinedly.

"*Well, you proposed to me,*" Fred thought. But he didn't say it out loud, as he watched Ethel pick up the phone and call Kyoto.

Papa-san nearly dropped the telephone receiver."You wish my lotus flower to *marry* the young man you've chosen to play Romeo!? And you won't even tell me who he is!?"

"That's right," Ethel assured him.

"Impossible!" Papa-san protested. He could think of a thousand reasons why such a thing could never be.

Five million dollars later, he was thinking he could always arrange a divorce at the proper time. Maybe even get a big settlement from this Groom.

"One down; one to go," Ethel congratulated herself. She picked up the ivory receiver again and then sat with it poised in midair.

"No," she thought to herself with the teensiest smile, "I really should see Jason in person."

A few hours later the formidable glittering Baroness was sitting on Jason's couch. Again Jason was highly appreciative of the Baroness's generous breasts and heady perfume. However, he, too, like Papa-san, was skeptical of her proposal at first.

"How can I marry someone if you won't tell me who she is?"

"But, honeybun, I have to be able to tell the press truthfully that you have no idea who you're marrying. That's what makes it so interesting."

"Of course, I don't want you to lie," Jason sputtered. "But this is my life!"

"Honey, you know how good I am at matchmaking. She's gorgeous, and, I promise you, you're made for each other." Jason admitted Ethel's reputation, but he still wasn't convinced.

"Believe me," Ethel said with absolute conviction, "she's the most ravishing young woman in the world."

Jason curiosity was definitely rising.

And then, to top it off, she added in a whisper, "I shouldn't tell you this, but I happen to know she performs a full half-hour of vaginal exercises, religiously, every morning."

"She what?" Buster was banging at the pearly gates, and Jason hadn't even let him out of his shorts yet.

"She performs a half-hour of vaginal exercises every morning."

"Oh!" Good God! Jason slumped back on the couch and let himself become dazzled by the concept. Why, he could almost taste it. He was still on a high from the Olympics, and now Buster was draining all the blood from his brain. Or was it the hypnotic glitter of the Baroness's diamonds? Between Ethel's psychic nips, and Buster's overactive imagination, Jason was a goner.

In a haze, he said Yes.

Back in Bev Hills, Ethel took stock. She'd nailed her Bride and Groom securely to the dotted line, with ruinous penalty clauses to ensure they didn't blab about being chosen. It was time to crank up the old publicity machine.

Ethel began by assuring her worried nearest and dearest that she'd found a *ravishing* young Romeo and Juliet the whole *world* would want to clasp rapturously to its collective bosom. Suddenly media bigwigs began perking up their sensitive ears. For, as we've mentioned, Ethel had a certain reputation as a matchmaker.

Said media bigwigs began assigning hirelings to sniff out the identities of Ethel's young stars. Ethel let the rumors buzz for a good month. Then she announced that her two ravishing young Mystery Stars would be married, *for real*, on the night of the full moon, during the filming of the movie's second-biggest scene. Two thousand guests–including the world's top thousand celebrities, come just to think of it–would be invited to the Ball and wedding. Oh yes, and Ethel would personally guarantee that, before the ceremony, the bride and groom would *never have met*.

An arranged star-studded wedding between two ravishing innocents on a night already chock-full of natural magic! It was just too romantic for words.

Ethel let it be known she was willing to broadcast the entire evening–wedding *and wedding night*–live. The networks went for the wedding, but reluctantly concluded, "We'd love to, but we just don't dare," to the wedding night. The cable channels had no such reservations, of course. And then there was the Interweb.

To top it off, Ethel dreamed up another outrageous surprise. She made a series of casual calls to a clutch of close gossip columnists and entertainment bloggers. "It's going to be *scandalous*!" Ethel hooted (yes, *hooted*). She concluded her performance by making each gossip swear not to breathe a word. By the following afternoon Croatian peasants and Tibetan sherpas were hotly speculating as to exactly how far Ethel was preparing to go. For half a billion or so smackeroos, the shrewd peasantry concluded, pretty damn far indeed. Rumors of the most extravagant stripe danced their way merrily out of the collective imagination and into the ever-cocked collective ear.

Mystery, as we've already pointed out, generates energy. And *nothing* about Ethel's extravaganza was known for sure.

It was media dynamite.

The scrapping for Cap Ball tickets was brutal. If you were a top "name," and you didn't find yourself among the two thousand lucky guests, you just arranged to bribe your way into a hospital for the weekend and primed your press agent to release breathless bulletins on how pluckily you were hovering near death and how distressed you were to have to let Ethel down.

Two days before the big event, Zelda arrived in L.A. with her attendant, Formerly Pretty Koko, and a contingent of ninja bodyguards.

I Luck Out. And In. And Out Again.

Zelda and her entourage were hidden in one of the guest cottages at the Bev Hills estate. Fred, Fifi and I were the only three Ethel let in on the secret of the Bride and Groom's identities. Fifi was indisposed, and Ethel wasn't about to let Fred get too close to Zelda, so she scheduled Zelda a session with me.

Zelda was the most desirable woman I'd ever seen–and I've seen thousands of women naked and moaning under my fingertips. The stories do not do her justice. I'm amazed that she found me as special as I found her.

I'm still not sure what happened. Within minutes, I was out of my right mind. I massaged her, and she danced for me, and then we ended up in bed. When we were ready, Zelda slipped a condom onto me, and suddenly I felt as though I were plunging deep within *myself*, into a bottomless Black Hole. I instinctively drew back–maybe too far back. With my eyes closed, clutching Zelda for support, I tried to reverse things by pulling out of the hole and going *out* as far as possible. Oops! I found myself zooming into outer space, into a huge Black Infinity that enclosed me *and* the Black Hole within. I fell back into that Infinity Within, which was so vast it folded around to enclose Zelda and me and all the outside Universe. Mutually Enfolding Infinities. There's no way to describe the sensation of pure awe. I awoke a child, discovering the world for the first time. Colors fascinated me. I was intensely aware of the smell, the taste, the texture of everything I was drinking in.

And I'd had a realization. I'd seen the Universe and knew where Einstein had gone wrong: he'd omitted from his calculations the two strongest forces in the Universe. $E=mc^2$ is only part of the story. Multiply the second side of the equation by the sex drive and the power of healing, and you shoot beyond the speed of light to where fantasy turns into reality, and miracles happen.

That day was almost upon us.

The Stage, at Last, Is Set

I had one day to recover from my night with Zelda. Tomorrow night would see the unveiling of the most amazing private residence ever built–a futuristic Taj Mahal, Fred's love-gift to his wife of forty years. The guests would include the world's top thousand megastars, dressed, overdressed or daringly undressed for a costume ball. A stunning mystery couple, chosen by the tingling nipples of the Baroness Ethelina von Elm, was going to meet for the first time onstage in the Grand Ballroom, marry, and proceed to a $7,000,000 Bridal Suite for their wedding night. The whole event was happening live on international tv and streaming internet video. And of course, it was all being filmed as the capstone of the Capulet Ball in Ethel's blockbuster remake of *Romeo and Juliet.* It was the Oscars, a Royal Wedding, internet celebrity sex tapes, the media event of the year–did I mention it was also Fifi's birthday?–and a few more stellar surprises, all rolled up into one. And I was going to be right at the heart of it all.

Or so I believed.

The Main Event
The Matron of Honor Prepares

Fifi awoke in her suite in San Francisco's Clift Hotel. Besides being Ethel's huge bash, today was also Fifi's 85th birthday. She enjoyed a whole slew of e-mails, flowers, gifts and phone calls, and then gave a free massage before lunch, as was her birthday tradition.

Right after, Fifi had to pull herself together and dash to Mr. Bruno's to have her hair done. Dying her whitish locks bright purple seemed such a good idea when Mr. Bruno and his giggling assistants talked her into it. Now, back in her suite, she supposed her hair *did* complement the low-cut crimson-silk gown Ethel had chosen for her to wear as Matron of Honor. After putting the dress on backwards only once, she managed to get it halfway zipped up. Around her neck Fifi clasped Ethel's birthday present–a gold necklace with "World's Greatest Masseuse" spelled out in diamonds. That Ethel! Fifi regarded herself in her triple mirrors.

"Good Lord," she sighed. Oh well, mostly it was the hair, and it was far too late to do anything about that now. She'd just have to depend on her charisma to overwhelm her ensemble. Still, wasn't there something missing? Ah, shoes. Her wobbly old pins having long ago rebelled at high heels, Fifi stepped into a comfy pair of bright-purple alligator flats.

Feeling just the teensiest bit like Cinderella, she took the elevator down to the lobby, climbed into the waiting limo, and said hello to the Mystery Best Man (not to mention any names).

"What have you been doing today?" she asked.

"Consoling Jason," I replied.

The Best Man Consoles the Groom

I'd awakened in my own Clift suite, called Fifi to wish her happy birthday, and then ordered brunch from room service. A worried Jason arrived just as I was scarfing down the last of my omelet.

"What am I going to do, Strange?" he wailed, as he guided me onto the couch and started undressing us.

"Do about–ooh, ah–what?" I wondered.

"Promising monogamy," he grunted, as he spurted all over everything. "I don't know how I let Ethel talk me into making this a real wedding. In front of billions of people I'm going to promise to make love for the rest of my life with only one woman. How can I possibly do that?" Neither of us could even picture it. Jason spent his life loving everyone he met.

"Wow!" I breathed.

"You said it," Jason agreed. "How can I love just one person? How can it even be *right* not to love everybody?"

And then it really hit me. "Even you and I can't…"

"Right."

Yeeks! This was our last time! I threw my arms around Jason. "This can't be!"

"I know. I've been worrying about it for days."

My whole inside felt empty. I'd assumed Jason and I…But Jason was a man of his word. If he promised not to have sex with anyone but his bride, that was it. An icicle stabbed through my empty innards.

"And I don't even know who she is!" Jason moaned.

I knew, but I'd promised not to tell. Oh my God! Another icicle stabbed through my entrails. Was I going to lose Zelda too? Arghh! Jason left around 2:00. I tried to console myself with the thought that I'd still be massaging half the megastars in Hollywood, but I was fretting at 6:00 as Fifi and I set out in the limo for Fred and Ethel's brand new Crystal Palace.

We were part of a mini-parade of special guests who'd been asked to arrive early–megastars who were going to perform, decoy Mystery Brides and Grooms, wedding attendants, etc. I got caught up in the excitement of it all, especially the thrill of being Best

Man in front of the biggest audience in the history of the world.

The limo purred across the Golden Gate Bridge and glided up the hill toward the Rainbow Tunnel that serves as the gateway to posh Marin County. Several miles later we turned off the freeway at the Lucas Valley exit and passed Skywalker Ranch. Sweet Georgie Lucas had colored lasers shooting up and reflecting off the clouds for miles around.

At last we reached the von Elm estate. The gate was modeled on the Arc de Triomphe, with, "WELCOME TO FRED & ETHEL'S MYSTERY WEDDING," in the arch.

"Like a McDonald's," I observed reverently.

Security at the gate was tight but efficient. Soon we were rolling through the grounds. Now what was this? There was a huge fountain off to the right, bathed in colored lights and spouting jets of liquid in time to music. Had Ethel bought the rights to Dancing Waters? How marvelous! Major money definitely had been spent.

Off to the left, huge letters made of colored lights seemed to be appearing in the air. "HAPPY 85TH BIRTHDAY, FIFI!" Well, wasn't that thoughtful of Ethel!

"Isn't that amazing?" I breathed. Then we rounded a corner and my mouth fell open.

We'd caught our first glimpse of Ethel's hush-hush new castle. It couldn't be! No! Impossible! We were going to drive right through what looked like a big pot of gold at the bottom of the hill, and then up a rainbow drive winding around the hill, to a spectacular Crystal Palace. I sank back, dazed. It was deja vu all over again.

"A pot of–oh, it's Ethel's rainbow theory!" Fifi piped up. Ethel had the notion, she explained, that people were concentrating too much on the pot of gold at the *bottom* of the rainbow, and thus were missing the wondrous delights at the *top*. "*This* from the world's second-richest woman!" Fifi concluded wonderingly. I was thinking Ethel had copied the rainbow-up-to-a-Crystal-Palace idea from my *Visioning* cover.

I was still trying to clear my head when we reached the main building. After being dazzled by the Grand Entrance Hall, we followed the crowd toward the Grand Ballroom, and found ourselves in a hundred-foot tunnel made of rainbows. I mean, it *was*. Lighting and dry ice mist and who knows what else had been used to perfect effect. We couldn't see the walls, the ceiling, the floor, or the source of the lights. Just wonderful rainbows–honest-to-God *real* rainbows–all around us.

And then the tunnel suddenly opened out into what looked like (to borrow an old line) the type of twenty-story Grand Ballroom God would have designed if She'd *just* had the money. The entire center of the room was a white-marble dance floor, above which was suspended what appeared to be an enormous mirrored ball, maybe eighty feet in diameter. Spiraling up the walls was a sort of rainbow slideway. Those who stepped on at the bottom wound up and up and then disappeared into a miniature Crystal Palace at the very top. Ethel was working this motif to *death*.

Fifi and I were escorted to an elevator which took us down one story. She was led off to meet the Bride in her dressing room. I was conducted to the Groom's. Meanwhile, upstairs in the Master Suite…

A Good Pink Fairy Frets

"Should I let the President come after all?" Ethel fretted. All afternoon, emissaries high and low had been urgently hinting that her country's leader, complete with fancy dress costume, just happened to have flown to the West Coast and could perhaps, if pressed, be persuaded to join her merry throng within the hour.

"No," Ethel decided. "Those Secret Service men are always just too tacky."

Besides, although she was certainly not a vindictive person, there was that little remark the Prez had made about her last year in Palm Beach. She turned her mind to more pressing concerns.

While a corps of dressmakers and hairdressers danced attendance, Ethel held a series of queen-size necklaces against her plump throat. "I think the diamonds and sapphires," she mused. Ah yes, they perfectly complemented her pink-silk Armani Fairy Princess costume. Oh, she was just going to *dazzle* her guests this evening.

Our Good Fairy tossed her head this way and that, making the filmy white streamers on her three-foot-tall pink-silk conical hat swirl merrily about. She tried out several effects she might use when she strolled casually out onto the Grand Ballroom stage.

"What do you think, Fred?" the Baroness inquired, revolving coquettishly in front of the mirror. She had to poke her lord and master in the ribs with her hi-tech magic wand to get his attention.

"What? Oh, fine, Ethel dear," replied the dithering Baron Frederick. The shortish plumpish Baron was feeling rather foolish in the outfit the Moon of His Delight had chosen for him. To complement her own Princess, she'd made her mate a Fairy Prince—yards of rich fabric and pounds of sparkling-but-sharp-pointed jewels.

"Oh, you didn't even hear what I asked," the Baroness pouted.

"Of course I did," the Baron lied stoutly. Then, making a shrewd guess as to what would serve, he added, "You look marvelous."

Ethel decided not to press the matter. She'd already concluded the necklace was perfect, and Fred was absolutely correct. She did look marvelous.

She gazed proudly out the window of her Crystal Palace's Master Suite at what a well-spent quarter billion could buy. From her tower apartment Ethel could see her whole real fantasy spread out below her. The entire Crystal Palace was made of priceless Laza-Glass®, which at the moment was glowing and flashing in intricate computerized patterns. The sight took her breath away. And there was a line of limos a mile long circling up the hill to her front door.

"I can't believe tonight is really happening," Ethel giggled. "They're just going to die!"

Ethel was not prone to delusions of grandeur, but a hundred years from now, she was sure, people would still be chitter-chattering about what was going to happen in the von Elm Grand Ballroom tonight. "Honestly," the Baroness thought (betraying her Texas roots), "I'm as excited as a polecat in a hen house!

"Time to go to work," she decided, a little shiver dancing up her spine. She pressed one of the buttons at the base of her magic wand. "We're coming down now," she informed the wand's tip.

"Roger," her left earring acknowledged.

"Come on, Fred," Ethel chirped happily. "Let's go 'greet the guests and meet the press.' And for God's sake quit fussing with your turban. And remember not to sit on your sword."

"Uh, you go ahead, dear," the Baron ventured. "I'm feeling a little queasy. I think I'll lie down for a few minutes."

Knowing her mate was just making excuses, the Baroness almost put her plump little foot down. But then she relented. Fred was always so uncomfortable in front of cameras, and you never knew what he was going to take it into his head to say. She'd do just as well on her own. She swept out of the master suite and descended to the hoopla she'd created.

As soon as the elevator doors closed, Fred ripped off his turban and wiped his perspiring forehead with the costly fabric encircling his forearm. The last of the von Elms, the most noble line on earth, was raring to plunk his heart at the feet of the young lady even his wife had agreed was the most desirable woman in the world.

The generally bumbling Baron Frederick von Elm, an uncharacteristically determined look on his face, scurried furtively into his Crystal Palace study. Fred's philosophy of life had always been, "Oh well." He was going to change that right now.

Once, as you remember, he'd done something daring. He'd defied his father and married Ethel. Now, a mere forty years later, he was about to do something daring again. Fred knew Zelda was the woman with whom he was destined to spend the rest of his days.

Oh yes, Ethel was wonderful. She had those marvelous breasts, and she had all those wild ideas. She made his life one merry madcap moment after another. Someone as timid as he would never have had the nerve to do any of those things on his own.

But maybe Ethel managed things a little too much. He was the second-wealthiest man in the world, but he was just a cipher in his own home. "Yes, Ethel dear." That was the extent of his contribution. And anyway–well, it really had nothing to do with Ethel. He was Romeo, and Zelda was his Juliet. It was as simple as that. You couldn't argue with True Love.

And, sure, Zelda was promised to Jason. But what was the use of being the second-richest man on Earth if you didn't use your money to buy what you wanted? Fred lowered himself into the swivel chair in front of his desk, and told his phone to dial Kyoto.

"The Baron von Elm is on your private line," the delicate slender young lady announced.

"Ah?" Papa-san Mishimoto looked up from the tv. Why would the Baron be calling? He hoped there wasn't a hitch with the wedding.

"Yes, Baron," Papa-san spoke into the receiver. "What may I do for you?"

"I want to buy Zelda."

"I beg your pardon."

"I want to buy Zelda."

"But Zelda is promised to another," Papa-san protested, while he did some rapid calculations. Zelda was to receive quite a hefty fee for her participation in the Baroness's movie, and then she was to return to Kyoto, much enhanced in value, to resume her regular duties. (Zelda's or Jason's wishes in the matter were not a factor.) So perhaps he should ask U.S. $10 million for her. "I could not possibly, er, sell her, as you suggest."

"How much?" Fred demanded.

"But, my dear Baron, one cannot sell human beings."

"I'll pay you twenty-five million."

"Dollars U.S.?"

"Yes."

"Fifty million," Papa-san countered. Perhaps he could get thirty-five.

"All right, fifty million," Fred answered instantly.

Papa-san cursed under his breath. He'd allowed his generous spirit to lead him astray. This fool Baron might have gone to a hundred. Oh well, too late now. "Agreed," Papa-san replied resignedly. "Where do you wish her delivered?"

Fred hadn't gotten that far in his thinking. "Uh, well, I'm not sure," he admitted.

"Does the Baroness know about this?" Papa-san asked.

"Uh, no."

Then the important thing was to get Zelda out of the Baroness' reach. "Why don't I have Zelda removed from your estate tonight and returned to Kyoto?" he suggested. "You can meet her here at your convenience."

Fred saw the wisdom of this arrangement. "Very good," he agreed. "I'll have the money transferred to your account immediately."

"I'll call Zelda and give her her instructions," Papa-san promised.

Luckily, Fred, with his electronic wizardry, had set up the security for the Crystal Palace. He was able to provide Papa-san with all the codes necessary to allow a helicopter to land behind the Palace. The arrangements made, Fred found himself stunned.

"Oh my God!" he said. "What have I done?" Then he hurried to Zelda's dressing room.

Zelda Prepares to Knock 'Em Dead

Satin-skinned Zelda, ravishing in filmy pastel wisps of nearly nothing, executed a graceful half-turn in the doorway of her dressing room. Her startling violet eyes were glittering, as were the various jewels scattered artlessly about her shapely form. From her left nipple dangled a gold ring supplied by the Baroness Ethelina. It was a Mobius strip, symbolizing Eternity, twisting on itself to form a continuous one-sided surface. The ring added just that perfect extra touch.

Zelda gave a happy toss to her jet-black waist-length perfumed tresses. She had, in effect, been preparing for this night since the age of five. In an hour she was going to dance at the triple-threat affair which had the whole planet bugging out its collective eyes, hanging out its collective tongues and exulting, "Zowie!"

In spite of all the pressure, Zelda was amazingly poised as she paused in the dressing room doorway to receive the homage of her little band of well-wishers. Her host, the Baron Frederick, devotion simply shining from every pore, bowed correctly and kissed her hand. Obviously he couldn't trust himself to utter, but his eyes said it all (or at least that portion of "all" of which the sheltered Baron was aware).

Zelda's attendants prostrated themselves. This, of course, was simply proper, but Zelda, flicking over them with a quick professional eye, was touched to note that this time they really meant it. And then Zelda's six ninja bodyguards prostrated themselves! The *ninja* prostrated themselves! For a moment Zelda almost lost her composure. What an unbelievable honor! What a tribute to the task she'd undertaken tonight! In a thousand years such a thing had never happened!

Like the Baron Frederick, Zelda could no longer trust herself to speak. However, if the Baron had not been shyly communing with his left shoe, and if her attendants and ninja had not been groveling on the floor, they would have seen that Zelda's unusual violet eyes, which even in ordinary times sent shivers up the spine, were positively strobing. Her chin was up, and she seemed to have been enabled by the great tribute which had just been paid her to look into a far higher and better realm. She thanked her well-wishers and asked Baron Frederick to excuse her, as she needed to prepare for her wedding. Losing his nerve, the Baron decided not to declare his love until after Papa-san had talked with Zelda.

With only Formerly Pretty Koko to attend her, Zelda stepped, with great dignity, into her dressing room. With a final incredulous glance at the prone ninja, she closed the door. "Great Buddha!" she sighed. Ah well, an hour of intense meditation, and she'd be ready. After such an incredible lift nothing could possibly go wrong. She was going to dance her Mininuko heart out tonight.

Zelda executed a few intricate ballet movements just to relax, and then twirled over to the shrine which always traveled with her. Settling into a comfy sextuple-lotus position (she was, you remember, triple-jointed), she closed her eyes and began the centering exercises.

Now, conceit in any form is absolutely abhorrent to a Mininuko. But it had suddenly occurred to Zelda that she might allow herself a sort of quiet pride that her humble self had been selected for this magnificent task. She was going to give the whole world a taste of Mininuko love. In the space of one perfect dance her viewers–humanity–would be transformed. Yes, she was quietly proud. Well, she'd better start her preparatory meditation.

Zelda closed her eyes again and attempted to empty her mind. Her mind had other ideas.

"I'm going to be married!" she thought. In any life, even (or, especially) a Mininuko Courtesan's, this is a major step. She tried to be thrilled. But she couldn't help thinking about Jason McVeer, the gymnast whose career she's been following so closely since she'd fallen in love with his image on tv. That curly white-blond angel hair. Those blue eyes. That supple body. That Rainbow Aura. She'd been glued to the set during the Olympics, and Formerly Pretty Koko had smuggled in Jason's *Workout Tape*. She'd never felt about any other man the way she felt about Jason. He'd become (well, practically) the only man she visualized during her own morning workout. She just knew he was the tree on which the cherries of her life should be hung. She hoped he was the Mystery Groom. The betting was that he would be. But what if she was about to marry someone else?!

"And," Zelda worried, "Is it fair to marry even a perfect stranger without his knowing what he's getting into? What will happen to him if I decide not to go back to Kyoto? Or if I decide to go back, for that matter?"

What would happen when her innocent new husband learned that Papa-san expected her to return to Kyoto and sleep with clients? There must be some way to escape from Papa-san.

"Would the ninja help me escape?" Zelda found herself wondering. "Or would they betray me to Papa-san? Surely after prostrating themselves…No, they were honoring the task, not me." But, still, you'd think…

And soon she'd be the biggest movie star in the world. Surely Papa-san wouldn't dare… "Yes, he would. And nothing could keep me safe if he put more ninja on my trail. Which he would."

No, she mustn't think about it now. Now she had to prepare herself for tonight's dance. That was all that mattered.

The first time she'd danced, as a little girl of five in a rude hut in the Amazon, she'd thought she was an orphan–an orphaned Goddess, but an orphan nonetheless. And during the dance she'd felt as though she could reach out and almost touch her true family, the other Gods and Goddesses in Heaven.

She'd since learned, or at least her mind had learned, that she wasn't a Goddess at all, just a human like everyone else. But childhood impressions aren't easy to erase. Her heart still believed she was a Goddess.

When the dance was going really well, she still felt as though she could almost reach... well, she still felt as though her real people were out there somewhere and she was *this* close to finding them.

It was silly, she knew, but that didn't make it any less real. Maybe it was the spirits of her real people who were out there somewhere watching over her. Oh, there was no way to put it into words. Sometimes she just felt as though she could merge with her real family in a way she knew was possible, but couldn't quite picture, even to herself. When she reached this tantalizing state she felt herself flooded with an ecstasy beyond anything she could attempt to name, and her dance became true Art.

But would it happen tonight? There'd be two thousand people in the Ballroom. She wouldn't be able to make direct eye contact with every audience member the way she usually did. Ah well, she'd have to trust to the inspiration of the moment. Other dancers might execute precisely choreographed steps. A Mininuko moved directly, freely, from her heart.

Right now she should put herself in the proper mood by closing her eyes and letting herself be filled with the secret loving feeling which, whatever its explanation, was the real reason she danced. She was just an empty vessel. Her job was to prepare herself properly. The rest was in the hands of the Gods.

Zelda's breathing slowed. Her eyes rolled back into the attendant sockets. Ah, it was working. She began to enter the timeless realm, where the energy of the dance could fill her.

Crash. F.P. Koko told her Papa-san was on the line from Kyoto with an urgent message. He informed her the arrangements had been changed. She could still perform her dance, but she was *not* to marry the Mystery Groom. Instead, the ninja would guide her to the pad behind the Palace, where a helicopter would be waiting to fly her to San Francisco International and a private jet to return her to Kyoto.

Oh no! Back to Kyoto?! Back to slavery! No gorgeous Mystery Groom! No movie career! NO! Zelda almost decided to defy Papa-san.

However, even if she did, Zelda might be risking death for nothing. Because...

Jason Still Has Cold Feet

Jason was in his soundproof dressing room studying his chest in the mirror. Clamped to his left nipple was a shiny Mobius-strip gold ring. It was Ethel's idea, and he had to admit it both looked and felt rather interesting.

He began running over his routine on the parallel bars. Let's see, a mount from the side, a snazzy stutz, a quick dip swing handstand pirouette, dip swing reverse straddle cut (adapted with a few surprise twists from the high bar), a glide reverse straddle cut, a Healy twirl to upper arms, back uprise straddle cut, etc., etc.

And topping it all off, his famous "McVeer triple spin reverse dismount." He could already hear the delighted cheers of EVERYBODY IN THE WORLD. And then he'd be marrying the Princess Charming chosen by Ethel's magic nipples. The thought definitely stirred him–especially one part of him–but mostly he was still desperate to escape. He'd never broken a major promise in his life, but he was thinking of, maybe not running out on the whole evening, but at least refusing to go through with the actual wedding. He just couldn't promise monogamy.

There was a knock on the door. It was his Best Man with good news.

"I had an idea on the way here," I told Jason. "To whom are you going to be making your vow of monogamy?"

"I'll be making it in front of the whole world."

"*In front of* the whole world, but only *to* your bride. Right?"

"Oh, I see what you mean. Right."

"And when you make a promise to someone, when is it all right to change the terms?"

"If they freely give you permission."

"You can go ahead and promise monogamy," I said. "I've met your Mystery Bride. I imagine she'll be willing to change tomorrow to an open marriage."

"But the whole world will know."

"You can tell the whole world you've agreed to a new arrangement."

The sun broke out on Jason's troubled brow. "You think so?!"

Just in case his bride didn't go for it, though, we decided to make love one more time. We were just helping each other back into our clothes when an attendant came to get the Best Man.

The attendant led me down the hall to a spot just under the center of the Grand Ballroom where Fifi was waiting. We were told to stand on a circular, six-foot-wide, white-marble slab with handrails, a hydraulic lift that would raise us right through the center of the stage. The big moment was almost here.

Behind the Palace, however, there was…

A Ninja Dilemma

Behind the Crystal Palace, the six ninjas who had been accompanying Zelda watched the landing of the helicopter Papa-san had ordered. Seiko stared at Nissan. Nissan stared at Seiko. "We must obey Papa-san," Seiko stated reluctantly.

"Yes," Nissan reluctantly agreed. It was a matter of honor, of face.

They could see no way out. A ninja is pledged to carry out all legitimate requests by the person who has contracted for his services. Papa-san was within his rights in demanding that Zelda be returned, forcibly if necessary, to Kyoto tonight.

Besides, if they didn't carry out Papa-san's order, the other ninjas would do the job and deal out punishment to Seiko and Nissan. The only possible alternative would be to flee with Zelda and then keep her hidden for the rest of her life. Even that might not succeed, and it would be no life for Zelda. She'd be better off in Kyoto.

"I wonder why he wishes her back tonight," Seiko mused. "Did he give no reason?"

"No," Nissan answered. "He just ordered that she be returned."

"Then we must do it," Seiko conceded sadly.

The Grand Ballroom Is Rocking

In the Grand Ballroom the giant hanging mirrored ball was reflecting the two thousand wildly costumed merrymakers below. It was the type of eclectic mix only Ethel could have achieved. Movie stars danced with housewives. Royals pushed frail folks in wheelchairs.

The Baroness was mingling with her guests when a voice in her earring announced that Fifi and I were in place. It was time for the Main Event. As the orchestra finished its number, Ethel boomed into the mike in her magic wand, "OK, Cowpossums, clear the dance floor. The wedding's about to start."

As the guests obediently moved to the sides, the backstage crews of five current Broadway musicals went to work. A fifty-foot circular section in the exact center of the floor was lifted hydraulically to form a stage. On it were quickly ranged modernistic thrones for the host and hostess and a smaller two-person couch. Onto the main floor around the stage were scooted fifty or so plush lavender crushed-velvet guest couches. A red-velvet rope on gold stanchions was run around this privileged inner circle. Then nearly a thousand pink, crushed-velvet, two-person couches were trundled in to cover the rest of the former dance floor. The whole operation couldn't have taken more than seven minutes. Then, typical of an Ethel affair, smooth precision gave way to mild chaos as the guests scrambled for seats. Luckily, none of the physically challenged were hurt in the stampede.

Trailing Fred in her wake, Ethel bounced out onto the stage, jewels flashing, lasers strobing from her breasts. "WAHOO!" she yipped with her famous Texas Ethelina yell. "Welcome, Cowpossums, to the Mystery Wedding of the Century!"

Beneath the stage, the slab on which Fifi and I were standing began to rise. We could hear Ethel outlining the evening's agenda.

"This evening Fred and I are throwing a housewarming for our new Crystal Shack, and we've invited a few billion friends to tune us in. We're also filming a little home movie. But most of all, we're going to be reveling in Romance. Two people who've never met are about to get married. My psychic nips have tingled up a bride and groom I know you're going to love. You've been moist with anticipation for almost a year. Your wait is almost over. Here they are, Cowpossums, the stars of our evening, our movie *and* our wedding. Help me welcome Our Mystery Bride and Groom, ROMEO AND JULIET!"

Mist rolled across the stage. Colored lights shot up. The mirrored sides of the giant 80-foot ball above the stage turned into high-resolution, full-color, 3-D video screens, magnifying what was happening on-stage. Then, out of the mist, rose the world's most notorious couple, the grandma/grandson erotic-healing team only recently sprung from charges of murder and prostitution. The crowd gasped, stunned at the sight of Fifi and me as History's Hottest Dream Couple. As the wave of shocked disapproval washed over us, my knees started to shake, and my lips went dry. I've never felt so ugly, so unloved in my life. It was horrible!

My inadvertent squeak for help must have summoned Ash-Kar. Suddenly, there he was, larger than life, sitting on-stage in a deep meditative trance. When there were no astonished gasps from the crowd, I realized that he must be invisible to all but a half-dozen psychically sensitive guests.

He smiled at me when he opened his eyes. Here I was, his own little pupil, at the center of such an enormous social storm! This was a familiar energy to him; he was used to being the eye of the hurricane. Of course, he'd been meditating on how to save Atlantis. Perhaps he'd find his Answer here?

Meanwhile, the crowd was horrified. Were Fifi and I for real!? This was what they'd been waiting for? NOOOOOOO! It had to be another one of Ethel's famous jokes. Didn't it? Only a few of the clearer-headed realized Fifi and I didn't even meet the requirement of never having met before. Sly Ethel let her guests squirm till exactly the right moment and then exclaimed, "Why, it's not our Bride and Groom after all! Here are our Matron of Honor and Best Man!" Ethel rode the wave of universal relief for a good sixty seconds. Then she invited the guests to give us a "warm loving round of applause" as she conducted Fifi and me to our on-stage couch. Aghast at their own rudeness, the crowd atoned with an overenthusiastic, if not exactly heartfelt, round of clapping.

Thankfully, their attention was distracted by the next performance. I watched Ash-Kar nod in silent appreciation as we all were treated to a half-hour of original music–sung, danced and played by the finest performers on Earth. It was incredible. As the last number ended, Ethel electrified the assembly with the announcement that now, at last, we were going to meet the real Mystery Bride.

Ethel pointed with her magic wand to the giant video ball above her head, and a ten-minute bio of Zelda played to an enthralled public. As the story ended, Ethel announced, "She's danced to please royalty. Now she'll be dancing to please you. Here she is, the most exciting woman in the world, our own Mystery Bride and the next Juliet, ZELDA MISHIMOTO!"

Zelda Rises

Zelda didn't see Ethel push the little button on her magic wand, but she did notice the dry-ice mist billowing across the hole above her head. Then there was a dazzle and rush of heat as the colored spotlights around her all came to life at once. Zelda continued to stand poised on the lift as it slowly began to rise. She felt supremely confident as her head poked through the stage and she caught sight of the cameras and the audience.

Said audience was entranced. The graceful female figure was rising through the dancing beams of light like Venus rising from the waves. Finally, Zelda, the Goddess of a billion dreams, stood poised in the exact center of the brilliantly lit white-marble stage.

Well, not quite *poised*. In truth, she was anything *but* poised. I hate to say it, but, through the wonders of modern technology, Zelda was about to make a complete fool of herself in front of billions of people. Zelda, and no one more surprised than she, had just come down with an all-capital-letters-and-four-exclamation-marks case of STAGE FRIGHT!!!! Stage fright, along with a most disconcerting feeling, akin to being a vulnerable virgin at a drunken samurai pillage. Imagine how you, yourself, would feel if it suddenly struck you that you were about to offer yourself as the intense erotic focus of far, far, far, far, *far* too many people. And far too late to back out now!

Zelda's dainty pearly whites suddenly began chattering like a women's bridge club on speed; her justly-fabled triple-jointed knees began knocking; and her lower lip commenced trembling in the manner of your own humble author faced with the prospect of honest work. All Zelda's internal organs seemed to be plunging pell-mell into her legs.

"Serene Buddha!" Zelda moaned. It appeared her love dance was going to be a tad less graceful than she'd hoped. Into Zelda's eyes sprang the wild look of purebred cattle being driven too rapidly uphill. What remained of her reason began desperately calculating her chances of being able to streak off the stage, race past the two thousand gaily costumed guests, twirl through the television and motion picture crews and leap over the rows of security guards.

No, in her present condition such a dash would have little hope of success. In fact, she'd be lucky if she didn't slump to the stage in about two seconds, slobbering and twitching like a fool. Besides which, for disgracing the Mininuko name so publicly, Papa-san's recently worshipful ninja would probably kill her on the spot, or hand her a sword and let her do it herself. What to do? What to do? What *could* she do!?

The crowd gasped. The alluring eighty-foot face that was staring right at them from the video ball was obviously in the throes of stark terror. This wasn't part of the show. She *couldn't* be acting. So, why was she terrified? Had she been frightened by something of which they themselves were about to become all-too-aware? For all these excellent reasons, they gasped.

Zelda saw an old man in magician's robes rise from a couch next to Ethel's throne and stride towards her. "Take heart," Ash-Kar whispered into Zelda's inner ear. "At worst you merely die." He topped off that comforting thought with a dash of pure pluck and energy, zipped directly into her crown chakra.

Zelda took a deep breath. She took one step forward. The flustered Baroness Ethelina signaled the orchestra with her magic wand. Music filled the hall. Zelda took another step forward. Her dance of love began.

At first she was hesitant, unsure. Her improvisational dances depended largely on the rapport she developed with her audience. She'd never danced before two thousand people. She couldn't look each and every one of them directly in the eye. She was used to establishing electric connections with each audience member and then playing with these zinging lines of contact. Tonight she couldn't do that.

But she could! The members of her audience were all watching home sets or, if physically present, staring at the eighty-foot ball. Zelda simply "played" directly to the cameras as she danced her own interpretation of "Love's Tender Awakening." Usually each of the twenty audience members had to be won with only one-twentieth of her attention. Now she could hone-in exclusively on whichever camera had the magic red light. The two thousand guests in the Grand Ballroom and the billions around the globe each had Zelda's undivided attention. Every one of us found the effect Devastating.

There's something about a vivacious young supposed-virgin saying, just to you, "I'm longing for Love,"–especially when she just happens to be the world's most refined courtesan. And then, when that ravishing young virgin oh-so-slowly awakens to the possibilities of Romantic Love–and just happens to have the most spellbinding violet eyes you've ever seen, both of which are staring directly into your very soul, positively dripping Love…Well, my heart zings just recalling the moment. Most of the world found itself *yearning* towards its various tv screens.

Zelda executed the slow intricate steps of the Copulating Tortoise for a too-brief eternity. She performed the graceful maneuvers of the Mating Swan. You can imagine. She segued into the rapid movements of the Rutting Rabbits. She did the Love Dance of the Fairies (Fred and Ethel's hearts fluttered).

Zelda felt herself being lifted, Lifted. She was Floating. Ahh. She'd left the Earth, transcended the realms of mere earthly desire. Now she was showing, not love, but Love. She was Dancing, not to the sounds issuing from the orchestra, but to the song swelling in her heart. Zelda felt herself becoming one with the whole planet, ready to lift off and return to her true Heavenly Home.

Billions around the globe connected directly to The Force.

Billions around the globe melted and yearned and fluttered.

For almost half the world, this was the first time they'd allowed themselves to feel intense desire for a woman. This acceptance unlocked blockages deep inside, allowing both the sex drive and the power of healing to flow more freely.

When Zelda finally slumped to the stage, spent, two thousand guests lay stunned on their couches for a full minute and twenty-three seconds. Then they rose to their feet and shouted their very lungs out, while pounding their palms into bloody little pulps. Billions around the planet whooped–yes, whooped–to their friends and families with joy. The entire world had been given an electric jolt of Love. The whole Earth glowed.

Zelda took her bows and was lowered on the little hydraulic lift in the center of the stage. Through a timing glitch, just as she was re-entering her dressing room, she caught a glimpse of Jason being led from his (he didn't see her). Her hero *was* her Groom! Back in her dressing room, Formerly Pretty Koko urged Zelda to hurry into traveling clothes and accompany her quickly to the helipad.

"No!" Zelda proclaimed. "Help me into my wedding gown." She'd decided to defy Papa-san.

Jason, meanwhile, was being guided onto the white-marble slab beneath the stage. He thought he'd been keyed-up the evening he'd won his fifth Olympic Gold, but now he felt as though his insides were being run through a Cuisinart. On the one hand he loved to perform before crowds, and the bigger the better. Two thousand people were Heaven. But there were so many celebrities. Plus, on tv, EVERYBODY IN THE WORLD. AND THEN HE WAS GOING TO GET MARRIED! It was hard to keep from tensing up his muscles.

When the applause for Zelda finally died down, Ethel proclaimed. "Now, at last, it's time to meet our Mystery Groom." She pointed her wand at the giant video ball. As soon as the crowd saw the circus baby with the big blue eyes, they knew the groom was their odds-on favorite. They shouted and veritably sang along to the remarkable saga of his life, and then Ethel declared, "You loved him at the Olympics. Now welcome in the flesh our own gorgeous Mystery Groom, your Romeo, JASON TOLLIVER MC VEER!" Mist rolled across the stage. The lift smoothly ascended.

Jason Also Rises

When Jason's curly blond locks appeared, the crowd went wild. The world had fallen in love with Jason at the Olympics, and the international media had fallen in love with Buster, the first pleasure organ the whole world knew by name. The public had seen photos and clips of Jason and Buster with somebodies and nobodies. Now here they were!

Jason was a little nervous as he went into his routine. However, he just concentrated on the feeling of movement–on the contest, the dance, between his supple young muscles and mankind's tenacious old adversary, gravity.

Yes! Jason had always relished physical stimulation of any kind. This was great! And, of course, everyone was watching. He was as aware of them as they were of him. Jason and the audience began breathing as one.

When Jason was balancing on the parallel bars, the whole crowd was balancing on the parallel bars. When he was flying through the air on the rings, they felt the freedom, the joy. Spontaneous applause arose. And then another point of interest did the same.

Jason's nervousness had vanished. He'd even became so exuberant he could look ahead to the latter part of the evening when he'd be marrying a woman who put in–and Jason never tired of losing himself in the thought–a half-hour of vaginal exercises each morning. And then he and his Bride were going to be the very first occupants of the Crystal Palace's $7-million "Honeymoon Suite," with *accoutrement* about which he didn't even want to think.

About which he *definitely* shouldn't have started to think. For one thing, it just played heck with his concentration (he almost slipped on the rings). For another thing, well...

Buster had never before, thank God, come up, as it were, in competition. But tonight, in front of all these important people, wouldn't you know it...

But was there ever a man who wasn't proud to have the whole world know he had a "big frisky one?" And let's get practical. He could hardly hide Buster in those tights. Jason just said what the hell. He let himself feel the smooth rings against his arms and hands, the silk of his costume sliding against his skin, the rush of air caressing him. As he finished on the rings and went into his finale, the floor exercises, that frisky god Pan, patron saint of abandon and revelry, took over his soul.

There was a luscious invisible partner rolling and tumbling across the stage with Jason. He could all but feel her, and he enjoyed her, without the shadow of a shame, to–well, the very utmost. The crowd found itself Marveling at Masculinity. As Jason performed his floor exercises, the entire audience was imagining itself a gym mat. As he finished, Jason's oh-baby blues stared into the camera with so much openness, friendliness and trust, so much pure shameless innocence, that the world fell completely in love.

For the other half of humanity (and you know who you are), this was the first time they'd allowed themselves to feel intense desire for a man. Again, this acceptance unlocked blockages deep inside, allowing both the sex drive and the power of healing to flow.

For the second time, the entire Earth glowed. A grinning Jason bowed and was led back to his soundproof dressing room.

The Ninja Fret

At the helipad, Seiko looked at his watch. Zelda should have joined them ten minutes ago. Deciding they'd have to go find her, the six ninja crept in a service entrance. Between there and the Grand Ballroom, they met and overcame a squad of security guards. Meanwhile…

On the Ballroom stage, Ash-Kar was still wondering how this Dream could save Atlantis. I was wondering if tomorrow would be too soon to find myself cavorting naked with Jason and Zelda together. And Fifi really, really, really had to pee.

Ethel strode to center stage and remarked, "I've promised you that the Mystery Bride and Groom would not know each other's identities until tonight. They still don't know. Each was kept in a soundproof room while the other was performing." She pointed toward the Ballroom entrance.

Spotlights drew the crowd's attention towards the Rainbow Tunnel. A fanfare of trumpets blared out. Fifty groomsmen and bridal attendants, half of them Megastars, filed in and ranged themselves around the stage. A little spaceship flew in, and the minister alit. In her most commanding voice our incomparable Hostess/Producer bellowed, "THEY STILL HAVEN'T SEEN EACH OTHER. HERE ARE OUR REAL BRIDE AND GROOM, OUR OWN SWEET ROMEO AND JULIET: ZELDA MISHIMOTO AND JASON TOLLIVER MC VEER!" She signaled with her wand. The orchestra swung into "Here Comes the Bride."

Out of the Rainbow Tunnel lumbered two freshly scrubbed, gorgeously dressed elephants. On the backs of the beasts were Jason and Zelda, both looking dazzling and adorable in white silk and jewels, and both blindfolded.

The ninja reached the Ballroom, seconds too late. They didn't dare abduct Zelda on-camera.

The elephants (Chauncey and Matilda by name) trundled up the ramp and onto the stage, where, with grunts of extreme concentration, they dropped to their knees, tucked their heads under, kicked their hind legs into the air and ended up in–ta da!–headstands. Jason and Zelda, for their part, slid easily to the floor and were guided to their places by their attendants. Chauncey and Matilda were led proudly to the side of the stage.

At Ethel's signal, Fifi and I removed the blindfolds. Zelda, of course, saw Heaven. For a fleeting instant Jason saw a Princess from Another Star, who morphed into the human Zelda. He was delighted. The participants and the billions of guests thrilled to True Love at First Sight. Hearts were fluttering as the wedding ceremony proceeded.

And then it happened. The minister asked if anyone knew why these two should not be joined in holy matrimony, and a voice yelled, "Stop!"

Rushing across the stage and kneeling in front of Zelda, the Baron Frederick von Elm, turban askew and robe tossed to the floor, blurted out, "I'll give you my entire fortune if you'll marry me instead."

Ethel's jaw dropped. Zelda grabbed onto Jason. The ninja, figuring the scandal was out of the bag, attacked the stage. The next ninety seconds zipped by in a blur. Zelda, an accomplished martial artist, engaged two ninja. Jason did a backflip off a passing elephant and knocked out Seiko. Another ninja ended up beneath said elephant (Matilda was no fool). Fifi dispatched the fifth with a sort of Vulcanesque death grip, and Ash-Kar pointed his Atlantean staff at the sixth, Nissan, who vanished in a puff (with a smile on his face).

Plucky Ethel, not willing to let a little attempted kidnapping disrupt her party, had the comatose ninja swept away, stared her errant husband back to his proper seat, and set the wedding back in motion.

Jason and Zelda panted, flushed with victory. Zelda's otherworldly violet orbs glowed, and Jason's oh-baby-blues sparkled, as the bride and groom looked each other up and down. Colored lasers strobed from eye to eye. The minister interrupted their personal light show to marry them with Mobius-strip gold rings, just like the ones Ethel had had them clamp to their left nipples.

When the minister announced, "You may kiss the bride," Zelda, giddy with delight, threw her arms around Jason's neck and delivered The Kiss of the Expert Young Courtesan Welcoming Her New Lover to the First of the Hundred Thousand Pleasures. She'd planned to do The Kiss of the Shy Young Bride Chastely Greeting Her Honored New Husband, but this was no time for artifice.

Jason's and Zelda's first kiss wasn't a little ceremonial peck. It was a real kiss. A very real kiss. And then more than a kiss. Well, Jason had no control, and Zelda was accustomed to making love both in and to the public. Within approximately thirty seconds, Jason and Zelda had slumped to the stage and were writhing around in a manner that could only be termed highly suggestive. The minister was clutching his heart and reaching out a blind hand for support.

The Honeymooners didn't even notice. There was no stopping Jason and Zelda. Buckets of cold water weren't even in it. It was obvious tons of court orders and teams of wild horses couldn't drag the young lovers apart. And who, indeed would want to?

Only Ethel; that's who. Prudish? Not our Baroness. But (as she muttered to Fifi) she'd "spent over $7,000,000 on a Bridal Suite to knock your sox off," and she was "damned if she'd see that sucker go to waste." She raced to center stage, shoved Fifi in the direction of the writhing Honeymooners and shrieked, "Mother, do something!"

"Wheek!" Fifi squeaked as she slid across the slick marble floor.

Fifi Falls into It

"Wheek!" Fifi felt herself skidding and listing to port. Luckily she was able to catch herself on Jason's and Zelda's heads as she sank to her knees. Automatically her right palm honed in on Jason's crown chakra. Her left groped for Zelda's. There. Whew.

Well now. My goodness. What should she do?

Fifi squeezed her eyes shut and condensed sixty-plus years of experience into her palms. And then she let it go.

Jason and Zelda ground to a sudden halt and lifted their heads. Jason felt sunlight pouring into his crown. Zelda felt her head connected to her Ancestors, to Heaven, to Home. To the two thousand in the Grand Ballroom and the billions around the globe, Jason's, Zelda's and Fifi's auras became startlingly visible. They watched as Zelda instinctively adjusted her vibratory rate to harmonize with Jason's and Fifi's. The colors of her aura changed to complement theirs.

Fifi, for her part, could feel something wrong with the way the colored electricity was zipping up and down Jason's spine. Well now "wrong" is the wrong word; because in Fifi's state nothing *could* be wrong. It's just that Jason's colored electricity seemed to be flowing less-than-perfectly-smoothly through his second, or sex, chakra.

Fifi had no idea why. Was it genetic? Could it be cured by surgery or drugs? Was it some prenatal or early childhood trauma which could be straightened out by years of intensive and expensive analysis? Fifi frankly had no idea. She just sort of wheedled some colored light through the area until the blockage popped. Jason felt a wonderful surge of sexual pleasure, but he didn't spurt. Oooooommmmmmmmmmm. The pulsing evened out. For the first time in his life he experienced an erotic charge that was slow and strong and steady.

Oh my God, he was cured!

Fifi, at that instant, shrieked, "Hairy Krishna!"

Hairy Krishna! Now that Jason's energy was flowing smoothly, Fifi recognized the feel of it. She hadn't felt it in sixty-odd years, but she knew it in an instant. She was feeling her own vibratory rate exactly replicated in another. Her precious old street-masseur/guru had reincarnated as a squeaky clean young gymnast. Jason *was* Bo-ku!

"Bo!" Fifi cried, peering down into Jason's face like a giddy old derelict suddenly spying free wine.

Jason had no idea why Fifi was screeching Bo at him, but he felt—well, he sort of felt as though he'd just spilled over into Fifi. Or as though she'd just poured right into him. They were closer than family, closer than lovers. Fifi! He was feeling toward her the way Romeo would have felt toward Juliet if he'd just let himself go.

Jason impulsively leaned over and pressed his lips to Fifi's heart. He felt such an immense surge of love for her that monogamy was actually forgotten. Jason unclasped the ring from his left nipple and started to offer it to Fifi. Then he saw Zelda, remembered he was a married man, and looked questioningly at his bride. Zelda was entranced. She watched the colored lights flash back and forth between Jason and Fifi. She wanted in on this! Fascinated at the prospect of sharing love with this remarkable, notorious old crone, Zelda helped Jason work the ring over Fifi's swollen knuckle.

The crowd recoiled, appalled. Oh, no! What was going on? Their golden fantasy was being twisted beyond recognition. Romeo and Juliet...and Fifi?

I felt a stab of jealousy in my gut, so hot I physically cramped. This wasn't right. *What about me? Choose me! You can't go without me!*

The Baroness whooped, "Good Lord! This wedding has turned into a three-ring circus!" She was delighted. More love! More healing! More scandal! More publicity!

My mind was racing. "*I belong with them. Why don't I walk over and join them? No, I don't dare. What if they don't want me? And the crowd will hate me. Yes, I should. No, I don't dare...*"

Fifi, however, wasn't aware of any of us. She looked into Jason's eyes and remembered her childhood Innocence. All the years of confusion and shame fell away. She lit up, with an aura that soon brightened to match Jason's. As the light around them intensified, their bodies seemed pale shadows of their souls.

The Ballroom filled with serpentine rainbows of light, curling around bodies, flashing off the mirrored ball. Each color seemed alive with sound and feeling.

Ahhhh! The crowd smiled and relaxed. They saw through their own silly prejudices. They actually welcomed Fifi into their hearts. The blockages of ageism were dissolving. For the third time that evening, pleasure-healing energy flowed, and Earth once again glowed.

Ash-Kar strode into the middle of the shimmering trio and ran his hands through their auras, absorbing their essences. At last, his Answer. He looked over and bowed to me, then with a happy sigh he closed his eyes and slowly disappeared. When he came to, he found himself lying on a white-marble altar in Atlantis, awakening from his Last Dream.

Ash-Kar Awakens

The temple floor was violently shaking. As Ash-Kar awoke, an elderly priest cried, "Praise the Being, you're back! Did you Dream? What is the Answer?"

"I Dreamed," Ash-Kar replied. "Now, if you'll leave me alone to ponder…"

"No time!" the priest urged, shoving a communications crystal at the blinking Godking. "WE'RE SINKING!"

Atlanteans across the trembling continent were linked up, terrified, waiting for an Answer. What could Ash-Kar tell them? How could anything stop the very Earth from shaking?

What was Ash-Kar going to say? How did his experiences with me and Fifi and Jason and Zelda have anything to do with Atlantis? What was the meaning of the Dream?

He racked his brain, but nothing came. Nothing. All Ash-Kar could think of was that he was here in this little chamber in Atlantis City. And all over the continent Atlanteans were now sitting with their eyes closed, their hearts in their mouths, and their communications crystals pressed shakily against their chakras.

"My fellow Atlanteans," Ash-Kar began, his voice and his image ringing in the minds of his desperate people. A moan went up as the populace, reading his feelings, saw no hope there. They faced the cold fact that Atlantis was Doomed.

Ash-Kar sighed and stopped his thinking. As he turned off his logical mind, images began to rise from the Dream.

One image was a rainbow staircase leading up from a pot of gold. If his people lifted their eyes up from earthly treasures, they'd see a Rainbow Staircase leading to Higher Things, to a Crystal Palace in the sky. Lifted their eyes. Lifting. There was something there.

Other images came. The dances on the Ballroom stage. Jason, Zelda and Fifi falling in love. Ash-Kar, joined mind-to-mind with the doomed population of Atlantis, began reliving those moments of ecstasy.

There was something in the way they'd loved…Ash-Kar focused on the sensation as he'd walked into the middle of Zelda, Jason and Fifi and run his hands through their auras. What had they been doing differently? Wait! Yes! That was it! Merging both the sex drive AND the power of healing. Why, that would double the intensity of their continent-wide orgasms...

Ash-Kar opened himself to the memory, and sent out to his people a powerful, loving, lifting image. Even as the final giant earthquake split the entire continent and the land began to sink into the sea, the spirits of the Atlanteans rose from their bodies. In a great energy-laden cloud they shot off into space.

"This way!" Ash-Kar commanded, thrillingly. He'd locked in on the Beacon. The great powerful all-comforting OM was there to guide them as the cloud of souls headed for the stars.

With Ash-Kar at its head, the soulcloud adjusted its direction, and, at nearly the speed of thought, began honing in on a peaceful planet circling Sirius B. Half the planet was sea. Half was brownish and greenish veldt, with giant red and green glowing pyramids the only artificial structures of any kind to be seen. And roaming over these pleasant plains were thousands of placid semi-telepathic hippo-esque creatures, with brains the size of peas.

One hippo-esque creature noticed something, and then, since all their minds were lightly joined together, they all noticed it. All over the planet hippo-esque creatures stared up at the sky.

Something new. They'd never *had* something new. What *was* this? It was a sort of cloud, a sort of mist. They'd seen clouds. They'd smelled mist. But this cloud mist was, somehow, alive. All over the planet hippo-esque mouths yawned open in surprise.

"Back into bodies," Ash-Kar ordered.

"What?!" was the indignant reaction from the fussy Atlanteans. "We descend into *those*?!"

Sirius B Joins the Party

Thousands of years went by.

And then thousands more.

One day, the Hiplanteans felt a warm glow from the direction of the planet they'd left aeons ago. Something was happening.

That very afternoon, as they locked protuberances once again and shot out into the usual communal cloud of bliss, their combined group essence was able to pick up the signal.

Earth was in the beginning stages of cosmic foreplay.

The cloud got so excited that it rained back down into its hippo bodies.

Protuberances began to wave again, responding to the signal. Colors swirled and focused. Colored beams of love were tentatively spiraled out to a Ballroom on the Blue Planet. Each ray that struck a receptive heart unlocked a secret.

Fifi recalled that innocent childhood game of "doctor," before she was taught sex was bad. Jason remembered expanding to love the "unattractive." Ethel thrilled to the joy of matchmaking the entire world. Zelda lit up as Ash-Kar intoned, "To experience true love, combine the best of sex with healing and forgiveness. Breathe, relax, accept love, give love, open…"

The foreplay was accelerating. Random members of the audience were startled with their own revelations. Jason and Fifi and Zelda were moving into connubial embrace. Jason laid out Fred's abandoned cape for them to lie on.

"Mmm, let's make love," he suggested to Zelda, tossing in the grin that had been his ticket to the Malibu beach pad of his very first movie star. "Fifi," he added, licking the back of her neck.

Fifi suddenly turned shy. She was all too aware that, through the wonders of modern electronics, all the teeming billions of her speciesmates were even now peering at Jason and Zelda and herself. In her impetuous youth, she had made love with Bo-ku in the gutter of a certain popular slum street in Delhi, with half the fascinated passersby either shouting hearty encouragement or hurling invective. And, she must admit, she'd enjoyed herself immensely. But then she'd been nineteen and healthy, and now she was…*nineteen*? she grinned, as a glimmer of something off in the rainbow spiral caught her eye.

The rainbow stairs didn't just spiral up from the ballroom floor to the top of the Crystal Palace. They also spiraled down from the ballroom floor into a lake. Fifi could see right through the shimmering crowd of people in various stages of embrace. And there, squatting on the shore of this otherworldly lake, was a sprightly young lady Fifi recognized.

"Lordy, Lordy, I'd forgotten!" Fifi cackled.

"I beg your pardon," the young lady inquired politely.

Oh dear, all at once the young lady seemed to be going hazy around the edges, and Fifi seemed to recall she had a message for her. "No time!" Fifi called. "Quick, you had a question. What was it?"

"What is my purpose in life?" the young woman answered, after a moment's hesitation.

Well, that's an odd one to have tossed at you by a perfect stranger, but it didn't throw Fifi. "Oh yes, holy masseuse," she advised.

"Wholly what?" the young lady called back.

"Well, fairly holy," Fifi amended, remembering some of the lighter episodes in her long career.

"What?!" the young woman pleaded as the lake began to fade.

Oh, the young Fifi hadn't heard. "Holy masseuse!" Fifi hooted as the young lady of the lake disappeared.

"What's wrong, Fifi?" Jason asked.

"Oh, nothing, dear. Just babbling to myself."

Jason returned his attentions to Zelda, who was lounging on the stage with a carefully considered portion of her raiment already fetchingly awry. And in her eyes was a look very similar to the one she'd unleashed at Akiru, her tenth love-suicide, the evening he'd committed *seppuku* for her.

Jason and Zelda fell into each other's arms, and Fifi didn't want to be left out, and soon Jason and Zelda and Fifi were all nattily attired in their birthday suits, stroking and kissing and loving. Now the world at large generally found itself peering intently at their screens and sort of *willing* the program director to switch to close-up.

"My very thought!" the program director agreed. But then she was faced with the dilemma, "A close-up of what and on whom?"

She figured she'd never be granted such license again. The home viewers found themselves switching rapidly among Zelda's talented breasts (one, nipple-ringed), Zelda's much-talked-about vagina, Jason's no-longer-nipple-ringed chest, or Jason's swiftly moving buttocks and/or Buster. Occasionally the viewers got to watch Fifi as, up from her shimmering pink heart, there leapt a beatific smile, a smile which just Ramboed its way out both her misshapen ears, threw out grappling hooks, and yanked the corners of her lips toward Heaven. She was grinning like Dear Abby on Ecstasy. Plus, Fifi as a whole was starting to glow. Oh, she was just *full* of energy.

"Shut your eyes," she directed her charges. Again, she plunked her right hand onto Jason's crown chakra, her left hand onto Zelda's. She opened her own crown chakra and let herself fill up with Power, Energy, The Force, The Source. Fifi directed Love and Healing through her hands.

Jason and Zelda smiled. All three of them sighed as one. They were in synch. It was time for…

A Consummation
Devoutly to Be Wished

Fifi crawled in between her two lovers. Jason's and Zelda's and Fifi's hearts melted into each other. Their bodies strove to do the same.

For real love, the experts say, go to a professional, and Jason had lucked into the world's two best. Best of all, Jason was no longer Buster's slave. Since Fifi had finally managed to zap erotic-healing energy through his clogged channels, he and Buster were partners, complementing each other, rather than working at odds. It was OK for Buster to enjoy himself. They could both just relax.

Jason still had the body and the training of a superb Olympic gymnast. Buster still had the enthusiasm. But now Buster no longer resembled an eager, goofy, Irish setter puppy. He'd grown (and was in the process of switching species) to become a powerful, confident, Arabian stallion. Whoa!

Then Buster grew even more and even more. Buster was a million miles long, and every inch was in ecstasy. And Jason was in control. He was in perfect control. Ohhh! Ohhhh! Aughooo! Ohhhh!

. . .

Zelda at last had found love partners worthy of her. All the subtleties she'd been wasting on her wealthy clients could be appreciated by sensitive Jason and Fifi.

Never had Zelda experienced anything like this. She was making love with a Young God in the peak of condition and with an incredibly subtle masseuse. She was being touched by hands that seemed to know more about her than she herself did. Whenever she moved, the response was instantaneous and absolutely perfect. She writhed into impossible pretzel shapes.

Jason's silky skin. Fifi's dry-and-wrinkled-but-touching-and-lovable skin. Mmmmmm. Mmmmmm. Zelda was floating, floating. Lights. Colors.

. . .

Fifi had found her darling Bo-ku again, her darling Prince Charming—and with Zelda as a bonus! Fifi was just overflowing with happiness. She let herself go.

Our favorite old crone was back with Bo-ku, with Bo-ku and an Indian Goddess (she couldn't remember her name). This Deity had a lot of arms, though, a lot of hands. Caressing hands were everywhere.

. . .

Eventually, without any of them reaching climax, the three Newlyweds subsided. There was no hurry. The original urgency had been soothed away. They had forever to lie in each other's arms, gaze into each other's eyes and love each other. It was impossible to watch without being moved, without finding your heart warming.

Jason and Zelda and Fifi were hanging on the balance point, the edge of Everything, the Door to Infinity. AND THEN THEY STARTED TO GLOW. We saw it onstage and on the giant ball overhead. Viewers around the world could see it on their screens. Light was pouring through the three of them, halos of light, klieg-lights and flood-lights of light.

Every civilization has its depictions of rapture and holiness, and they all show light glowing around the holy ones' bodies and heads. Here it was, for all the world to see.

Light was pouring out of their eyes. And their eyes were searching...for something...or someone...

The three of them were now vibrating in perfect harmony. And it was bliss. However, they were now sensing, together, that someone else had almost exactly the same vibratory rate, someone close by. Who could it be?

As their fabled third eyes opened, they peered around. Ah! Ah! There! On a couch just across the stage. Another partner. No, not Ethel...

MOI!

I was still lying on my double couch, staring mesmerized across the stage. At first, I'd been *aching* to be with my three lovers, at the center of the stage, where I *knew* I belonged. Seeing them so close but out of reach had been tantalizingly frustrating. Didn't they know I should be with them?

And then, as my heart began to melt and glow, the jealousy subsided. I focused, not on myself, but on the love that I felt for each one of them. Jason, who had shown me how to be spontaneous and innocent and free...Zelda, who had opened her body to offer me the cosmic secrets that she carried...And dear old Fifi, my long-lost grandmother, from whom I had unknowingly inherited so many of my quirky skills and fascinations...

How dear these beings were to me! How very much I loved them all!

The more I focused on the love, the better I felt. As I released my neediness and fears, my own heart opened. My mind cleared. My vibratory rate began humming along.

And now Jason and Zelda and Fifi were turning towards me, reaching out welcoming arms. Zelda was unfastening her nipple ring, my wedding ring, and holding it out to me. With a cry of joy I raced across the stage. "I DO!" I yelled. And I shoved that sucker onto the third finger of my ever-ready left hand. *I was a married man!*

And Then We Were One

With that, I, too, began to glow. Dear Reader!

I'd experienced brief instants of Light. But this was a strong, steady, powerful glowing. Jason and Zelda and Fifi and I were all glowing together. We were becoming a unit, an Instrument. We could do something with all this Energy.

We became aware that something was still missing, still incomplete. But what could we have overlooked?

Jason and Zelda and Fifi and I loved each other with a love that was not possessive. We wanted each of us to love all of us. That each of us tried to do so was what we loved most about each other. And that each of us tried to love everyone. Yes! That was what was missing. US LOVING EVERYONE. EVERYONE LOVING US. EVERYONE LOVING EVERYONE.

We wanted to share this incredible Glory that was filling us to overflowing. Sharing it wouldn't dissipate it, but would only make it even more powerful, even stronger.

Jason and Zelda and Fifi and I stood in the center of the Grand Ballroom stage and opened our arms to the world. On a level higher than the physical I felt my new spouses with me, next to me, surrounding me. Jason and Zelda and Fifi and I were all together, shining, holding out our arms.

We all began speaking at once. "WE LOVE YOU. FEEL FREE TO LOVE US, FEEL FREE TO LOVE EACH OTHER. LOVE IS EVERTHING. LOVE IS ALL." The message was clear to any who wanted to see it, to hear it, to smell, taste, and feel it.

The guests in the Ballroom were hungry for this. For weeks, for months, they'd been anticipating great, extravagant romantic love. For hours they'd been actually seeing it–starting with gorgeous young lovers, then expanding to include Fifi in their fantasy, and then me. They'd seen love grow to Love. They'd watched us all Light up.

Ethel had gathered in the Grand Ballroom some of the most highly charged, electric people on Earth. Two thousand strong. Megastars and dying folks, hearts overflowing, began to fall into each other's arms–some sexually, some platonically, some laughing, some crying. Some went for two out of three, or three out of four.

They began to Light up too.

They were the tinder that set off the wildfire. All around the world viewers watched us loving, glowing. There is a level on which all of us are joined, and we were touching it. The fire began to build. Humanity felt its collective Heart opening.

The entire world exulted, "YES!" Love was just surging from the Ballroom, and pulsing all around the globe. Billions reached towards climax. The whole planet glowed.

LIGHT! LIGHT! The whole world was reaching slowly, luxuriously, toward LIGHT!

The radiance was so pure, even the psychic hippos on Sirius B looked up from their endless lovemaking.

The Universe was shaking. Shuddering. Like Atlantis had.

Beams of light shot from Earth and ignited the Milky Way.

The trembling became uncontrollable.

We abandoned ourselves to loving everyone and everything.

And then, for the first time ever, the entire Earth burst into an...

Orgasm

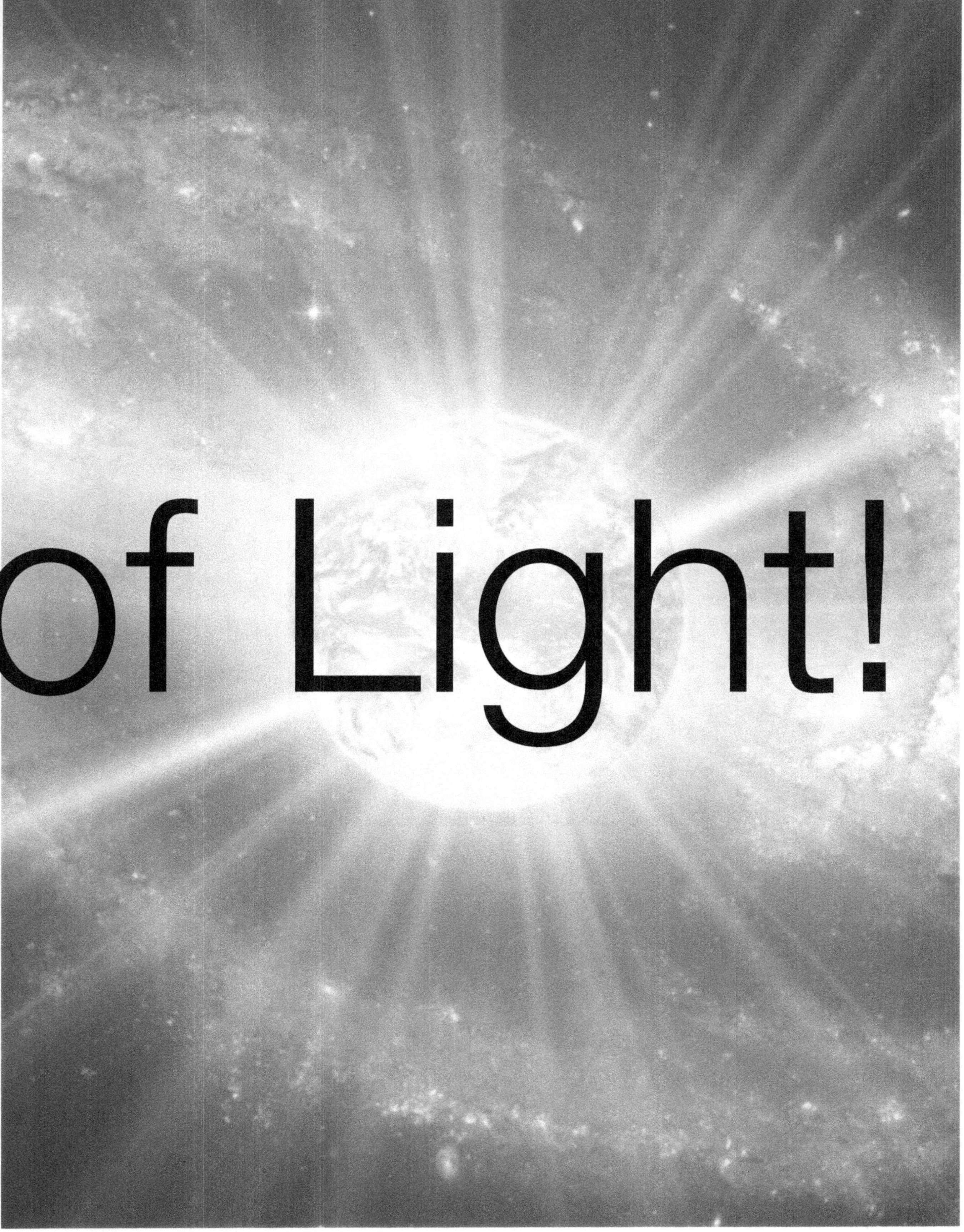
of Light!

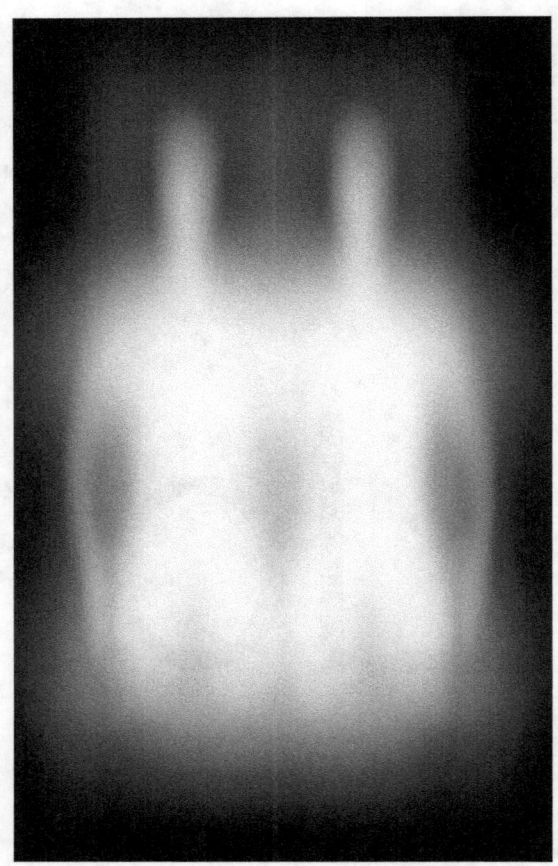

An illuminated thanks to my
impeccable editor David Cates
and
visionary designer Jeff Byers

Acknowledgments

Thanks also to Stephen Pullis, my roomie for almost twenty years; to Jake Vreeburg and Tom Boyer; and to my brother, sister-in-law, niece and nephew.

Thanks in alphabetical order to Wilkes Bashford, Chris Baxter, Bruce Bellingham, Peter Berlin, Burly Jed Boothby, Peter Bothel, Ashleigh Brilliant, Jim Boudinot, Matthew and Po Bronson, Judy Brown, Michael Brown, Mayor Willie Brown, Mike Brownstone, Mark Burstein, Christopher Caen, Cher, Alan Clark, Joan Collins, P.J. Corkery, Bob Craft Sr., Hank Donat, John and Pagel Dvorsek, Rob Epstein, Rupert Everett, Dave Ford, Tom Flesher, Rink Foto, Roberto Friedman, Leah Garchik, Rick Gerharter, Donal Godfrey, Herb Gold, Janis Greenberg, Harry Helbing, Deirdre Higgins, Martin Hyland, Andrea Jacobson, Angelina Jolie, Cleve Jones, James Patrick Kennedy and Derrick Tynan-Connolly, Scrumbly Koldewyn, John Kyrk, Michael Larsen and Elizabeth Pomada, Mark Leno, David Letterman, Lisa de Longchamps, Madonna, George Maguire, Stan Maletic, Ken Maley, Abbi Marchesani, Rick Mariani, Armistead Maupin, Dream de Menthe, Bob Meslinsky and Phil Diers, Bette Midler, Liza Minnelli, Peter Mintun, Rumi Missabu, Marcus Mitchison, Pat Montandon, Christopher Moore, Ed Moose, Tom and Cindy Morse, David Murdock, Michael Musto, Andrew Nance, Dr. John Newmeyer and his sister Mz. Julie Newmar, Mayor Gavin Newsom, Dan Nicoletta, Charlie Peer, Emo Philips, Michael Phillips, Brad Pitt, John Poultney, Terry Pratchett, Mark Rubnitz, Tom Ruge, Steven Saylor, Yahoo Serious, Charlotte Shultz, Mz. Beth and Corey Silver, Gregg Slapak, April Smith, Michael Smith, Stefan Smith, Parker Stevenson, Sweet Pam Tent, Patrick Treadway, Todd Trexler, Dede Traina, Robert Triptow, Carole Vernier, Randy Warder, Robin Williams, Sean Wilsey, Cintra Wilson, Henry Winkler, Daric Wolkenhauer, Sam Yap, Michael Zambotti, Merla Zellerbach and Danny Zielinski.

And, of course, I'm tremendously grateful to Herb Caen, Cal Culver, Lady Jane Montgomery, Andy Warhol and Dame Edna Everage. Special thanks to Ash-Kar, my formerly imaginary Spirit Guide, and to thousands of massagees.

Bless you all.

For the promised free text of *Visioning*
and for all the events too peculiar to squeeze into *Billions of Virgins in Ecstasy*,
visit

www.StrangeBillions.com

About de Author

You've probably realized part of my story is fictional. Frankly, I assumed most of it was.

However, if you'll Google the *San Francisco Chronicle* for January 23, 2004, you'll find a three-page story entitled "Strange but true," revealing that, like me, Real Strange had been a simple San Francisco town-fool/masseur since 1972, and, like me, had written *Visioning* (Ash-Kar Press 1979), *The Strange Experience* (Ash-Kar Press 1980), and the photo history *San Francisco's Castro* (Arcadia Publishing 2003).

Now I don't know what to believe.

www.ingramcontent.com/pod-product-compliance
Lightning Source LLC
Chambersburg PA
CBHW081153170626
46813CB00009B/3182